James Madison Mathes

Letters to Thomas A. Morris, D. D.

James Madison Mathes

Letters to Thomas A. Morris, D. D.

ISBN/EAN: 9783337274764

Printed in Europe, USA, Canada, Australia, Japan

Cover: Foto ©Andreas Hilbeck / pixelio.de

More available books at **www.hansebooks.com**

LETTERS

TO

THOMAS A. MO

Senior Bishop of t

BY

JAMES M.

A MINISTER OF THE

this rock I will build
hades shall not prevail

CINCINNATI:
PUBLISHED FOR THE AUTHOR
GEO. B. DERBY & CO., PRINTERS.
18__.

PREFACE.

The first ten of the following series of Letters were published in the "Christian Record," commencing in November, 1859. In this way they were widely circulated and extensively read by the Christian brotherhood, and others who felt an interest in the important issues discussed. When we reached the tenth number in the series, we became satisfied that we would have to place them in tract or book form for general circulation. The voice of the brotherhood, as conveyed to us in numerous letters, seemed to demand this; and we yielded to the wishes of many brethren and friends.

These Letters as published in the "Record" produced quite a sensation upon some of the friends and admirers of Bishop Morris. We heard of one case, where a member of the M. E. Church borrowed the "Record" containing one of these letters, and when he had read it, he became so much excited that he threw it into the fire, in order to destroy the letter!

But this was an exceptional case. We have abundant evidence that many were induced, by reading these Letters, to search the Scriptures, and were led to embrace the truth. We have therefore added several new letters to the series, and revised the ten that appeared in the "Record," and now offer them to the public in this little volume, which is cheap and within the reach of all.

Let no one throw it aside, as unprofitable, because it

is *controversial.* It is true, we have called in question many of the positions taken by the good Bishop, and fully sustained our objections, by the admissions of the most learned and able men in the M. E. Church and by Scripture testimony; but in doing so we have abused no one—we have always endeavored to distinguish between the *system* and the honest people who embrace it. We have used hard arguments and pleasant words, and trust that we have manifested the Christian spirit.

Our object has not been to wound the feelings of any one, but to arouse them to search the Scriptures. We love the good and honest of all denominations, and desire to see all united upon the "one foundation" according to the prayer of the divine Savior. Such union can not be consummated until sectarianism is made to give place to Christianity. Men must be brought to love God and the Bible more than party, before they will consent to such a union.

If these Letters should prove a means, by the blessing of God, of leading any to a candid investigation of the great issues involved, in the light of the word of God, we shall be fully satisfied that our labor has not been in vain. The blessing of God attend all who desire to know the truth!   TFE AUTHOR.

LETTER I.

Introductory—Under what circumstances we became acquainted with him—Read his book with interest—Buy the Discipline every four years—The Bishop's mature thoughts—The text very appropriate—One in spirit, though they may differ in speculative theology, forms of discipline, etc.—No sectarian or party names in the primitive church—Dr. Morris mistaken—The primitive Christians were all one—Dr. M. teaches that division is not incompatible with unity—Paul teaches that division among Christians is carnal—Are the Methodists one in heart with the other sects?—Calvin and Servetus differed in "speculative theology"—Were they one in heart?

THOMAS A. MORRIS, D. D. :

My Dear Sir—A short time ago I saw it announced in your church organs, that a book was in press written by you, being a discourse delivered by you before the North Indiana and Pittsburg Conferences, both of which took action, requesting its publication ; and entitled,

"A Discourse on Methodist Church Polity. By T. A. Morris, D. D., senior Bishop of the Methodist Episcopal Church."

I determined to procure the work as soon as

it came out; and I have been fortunate enough to succeed. I was very anxious to read your book, from the fact that I have long known you by reputation, and I was introduced to you, and spent a very pleasant afternoon with you and other friends, at the house of our mutual friend, Hon. Joseph A. Wright, then Governor of the State of Indiana. This I think was in the winter of 1853. I was then much pleased with your frank and manly bearing, and delighted with your candid and edifying conversation.

These circumstances, together with the fact that you are the senior Bishop in your church, prepared me to read your explanation and defense of "Methodist Church polity," with candor, and without prejudice. And I may say to you, Doctor, without flattery, that I count myself happy in being permitted to study Methodism under so great a master.

It is true, I have read the writings of most of the great men of your church, such as Wesley, Clarke, Fletcher, Benson, Watson, Inskip's Methodism, and Jonathan Crother's "Portraiture of Methodism." I have also read and studied your Discipline, getting a new one every four years, in order to keep up with the changes and reforms made upon it by the General Conference. I have also been a pretty constant reader of the *Western Christian Advocate* for many years, and of course from all these sources of information I had enjoyed a fair opportunity of becoming acquainted with Methodism; but still, I read your little book with peculiar interest.

Having finished the reading of your book, I have concluded to review it, in a kind and Christian spirit, in a series of Letters. I shall use pleasant words, and hard arguments, in opposing what I consider wrong in your discourse, or in Methodism as you explain and defend it. You have said some excellent things, and have said them well, and in a very plain and forcible manner, for which I award you all praise. Yet you have said some things to which, with the Bible in my hand, I am compelled to enter my protest.

This little book, you assure us, contains your "mature thoughts" on your church polity. No one acquainted with you will doubt your candor, or your ability to develop your church polity, and prove it to be of divine authority, if indeed it is so. Your book must therefore be received as a standard work, upon the subjects upon which it treats.

You have taken a very appropriate text. Let us repeat it: "For though I be absent in the flesh, yet am I with you in the spirit, joying and beholding your order, and the steadfastness of your faith in Christ ;" Col. ii. 5.

After reading your text, you say, by way of introduction : "This Epistle of Paul is addressed 'to the saints and faithful brethren in Christ which are at Colosse,' or to those who not only profess Christianity, but faithfully practice its precepts and experience its saving power. All such are one in spirit. They may differ in speculative theology, in forms of discipline, modes of worship, and in name, but they are one in heart."

We most cordially agree with you that the church at Colosse was a model church, not only professing the religion of Jesus Christ, but faithfully practicing its divine precepts and experiencing its saving power. But your next statement we can not receive. How do you learn that the Colossian brethren differed in speculative theology, forms of discipline, modes of worship, and in name ? Were they divided into Trinitarians, Arians, Unitarians, and Materialists, and still *one in spirit?* Were they divided in name, as Methodists, Baptists, Presbyterians, Lutherans and Quakers ? Did some of them adopt the Discipline of the M. E. Church, another party the Westminster Confession of Faith, while others walked by the various rules of the Baptists, Lutherans and Quakers? I know that you will not claim that such was the case in this model church at Colosse. Will you affirm that such a state of things existed in the primitive church? Were they Methodists at Jerusalem, Baptists at Rome, and Presbyterians at Corinth? No indeed, you know that no such divisions existed in the primitive church, and for many hundred years after the death of the Apostles.

From what premises then do you draw your conclusion, that Christians may differ as you say above, and still be one in spirit? Does Christ or the Apostles intimate in a single instance, that Christians might be one in heart, while differing in "speculative theology, forms of discipline, modes of worship, and in name?" Certainly, nowhere in the New Testament can such an intimation be found. But on the contrary, Christ prayed for his followers, "That they all may be one, as thou Father art in me and I in thee, that they may be one in us;" John xvii. 21. Paul says, "Now, I beseech you, brethren, by the name of our Lord Jesus Christ, that ye all speak the same thing, and that there be no divisions among you; but that ye be perfectly joined together in the same mind, and in the same judgment;" 1 Cor. i. 10.

Thus you see that Paul and his Master were both opposed to such division as you say may exist, and still the parties be one in heart. And with them agrees every inspired writer. No, Doctor, you are mistaken. It is a naked assumption, without a shadow of authority from the oracles of God. You see professed Christians now differing in all these particulars, and in the goodness of your heart, you wish to excuse them, and throw over them the broad mantle of your charity, and, therefore, *assume* that these differences do not hinder them from being *one in heart.*

Let us look at this a little further. Your language, although perhaps you did not intend it, is calculated to make the impression upon the casual reader, that you had found in the church at Colosse, a model for all the division you mention. You say "All such are one in heart." "They may differ," etc. I need not say to you, because as a Bishop you know, that not only the Colossian church, but all the primitive Christians walked by the same divine rule, the word of God, and all wore the same worthy name—the name Christian, from Christ their head and husband, which was given to the disciples, first at Antioch, by divine authority.

As to their order of worship, Luke tells us,

"They continued steadfastly in the Apostles' doctrine and in fellowship, and in breaking of bread, and in prayers." No division there, Doctor. The great apostle Paul differed with you amazingly in his estimate of division. You teach us that division is not incompatible with *unity*, and the spirit of Christianity; while he rebuked the manifestation of the spirit of division in the Corinthian church, by saying, "I could not address you as spiritural, but as carnal." "For while one says, I am of Paul, and I of Apollos, and I of Cephas, and I of Christ. Is Christ divided? Was Paul crucified for you? or were ye baptized in the name of Paul?"

Paul teaches that where such division exists, the parties so divided are "carnal and walk as men." While you teach that such differences may exist, among professed Christians, while they may still be *one in heart*, and "spiritual." Who shall decide when doctors disagree? For myself, I prefer Dr. Paul, much as I love and admire Dr. T. A. Morris. And until you produce some better authority for division and sectarianism than your mere *assumptions*, I must continue to adhere to the old notion, inculcated by Christ and his Apostles, that union is *divine*, and that division or sectarianism is *heresy!*

But is it so in fact, Doctor, that the differences you speak of do not break fellowship? Are the Methodists "one in heart" and spirit, with all other sects and parties? If they are, then we have been mistaken all our life; and if not, then your language is calculated to mislead. You are a Trinitarian, and differ in "speculative theology," from Unitarians, Arians, Socinians, Pelagians and Universalists. Are you all one in spirit and in heart, notwithstanding these differences?

John Calvin was a Trinitarian, and Servetus differed with him in some little matter of "speculative theology;" yet Calvin had him burned at the stake for this difference! Were they one in spirit and in heart? *Credat Judaes Appella; non ego!*

LETTER II.

Importance of the word of God as a rule of faith—All profitable, and therefore essential—Stick to it for life—If wrong, change—Paul changed—Apollos changed—Martin Luther changed—The "Iron bedstead."

THOMAS A. MORRIS, D. D.:

My Dear Sir—I see that you only make two points in the discussion of your text, viz. :

1st. Faith. 2d. Order. We only propose to examine a few things under your first head.

On page 10th, you say: "And here we endorse for every consistent Christian that he believes all Bible truth, especially all truth essential to vital Christianity."

Now, sir, from the above statement, I infer that you do not hold all "Bible truth" to be essential to Christianity! That you hold to two classes of "Bible truths," one *essential*, and the other *non-essential*, and that even a good Christian may disbelieve the non-essential truths of the Bible without endangering the *vitality* of his religion !

But the great apostle Paul differs from you upon this subject. He says, "All Scripture given by inspiration of God, is profitable for doctrine, for reproof, for correction, for instruction in righteousness : that the man of God may be perfect, thoroughly furnished unto all good works ;'' 2 Tim. iii. 16, 17.

According to your statement, Doctor, some truths in the Bible are not *essential*, and are consequently *"unprofitable!"* But according to the apostle Paul, it is all *profitable*, and therefore *essential*. Our best lexicographers define the word essential to mean "necessary to." Any Bible truth that is not necessary to vital Christianity is non-essential, and vital Christianity would be just as perfect in every respect if all such non-essentials were left out of the Bible entirely ! Such non-essentials are not profitable for doctrine, for reproof, for correction, for instruction in righteousness, and can be of no value in making the man of God perfect unto all good works. Simply because they are *unnecessary*—*" non-essential"* to vital Christianity ! Are you prepared for this, Doctor ?

2. The next objection I have to your statement above is, that you seem to have two sorts of Christianity ; the one you call *"vital* Christianity," and the other I suppose is a *lifeless* or dead Christianity ! Where in all the book of God do you read of " vital Christianity ?" We had, in our simplicity, always supposed that the Christianity established by our Lord and his

inspired Apostles, was a living Christianity, and that every thing taught by Christ and his inspired teachers was essential to it! Have I been mistaken? It would seem so, if you are correct. But I know I am not mistaken, when I affirm, that whatever claims to be from Christ that is not *vital* is a forgery and a libel on true Christianity.

3. Before leaving your first head, you say : "Before we adopt any system, we should be satisfied that it accords with the Bible, and then stick to it for life."

Now, my dear Doctor, I must be permitted to differ entirely from you upon this point. There is not an honest sectarian in the land, no matter how heretical his religious creed may be, who is not satisfied that his "system accords with the Bible!" And the more ignorant he may be of what the Bible plan of salvation is, the more confident and dogmatical is he in affirming that his "system accords with the Bible!" Yet, you would say to all such ignoramuses, because they are honest in their views and impressions, *stick to it for life!* But I would not. I would, however, give all such the instruction of the Savior, "Search the Scriptures, for in them ye think ye have eternal life, and they are they that testify of me."

You and I both believe that the Calvinistic "system does not accord with the Bible," but is contrary to it, and subversive of its teachings ; and yet we know that thousands, both in Europe and America, honestly embrace it, and are satisfied that it accords with the Bible. Yet, you would advise them to "stick to it for life," notwithstanding you oppose it in your preaching, and regard it as a dangerous heresy ! A system which the eccentric Lorenzo Dow has reduced to an absurdity, thus :

"You can, and you can't,
You will, and you won't,
You shall, and you shan't,
You'll be damned if you do,
You'll be damned if you don't."

But still you would advise the honest Calvinist to "stick to his system for life"—to search no further—investigate no further—but "stick to it for life."

4. But I will tell you, Doctor, what course I take with all honest Calvinists, and all other honest persons whom I find in error, and satisfied to remain so ; I would advise all persons, no matter how well satisfied they may have been when they embraced their religious systems, to "Search the Scriptures"—"Grow in grace and in the knowledge of the truth"—"Be not un-

wise, but understanding what the will of the Lord is." And if in the progress of their investigations they should learn the "way of the Lord more perfectly," and as a consequence discover that the system which they had hon‐ estly entertained for years as according to the Bible, and with which they had been satisfied, was *wrong*, I would advise all such to *change*— give it up, and "stick to it" no longer, but set themselves right without any unnecessary de‐ lay.

It is the duty of every man to embrace that system which not only *accords with* the Bible, but which is actually taught in it. This advice I would give to every sectarian in the land. No matter how long he may have been satisfied with his human systems, nor how prominent he may stand in his *branch* of the sectarian tree ; even if he has been dubbed " D. D." or " Bishop," (in the modern sense,) I would urge him to read and investigate, and if he finds that he has been mistaken, give it up. Let him not dare to "stick to it for life," through personal pride, or vain glory, but make haste to change, as an honest man convinced of error.

I know it is pretty hard for a popular man, and especially a preacher, who has been identi‐ fied with a cause, or system, to give it up, and

2

frankly and honestly say, *I was wrong.* There are many little reasons which a man may use to quiet his conscience, so that he may "stick to the error for life," though convinced that it is an error.

When I was a student at the University, I was intimately acquainted with a Presbyterian minister, a Doctor of Divinity and a Professor. He had been satisfied that the system taught in the Westminster Confession of Faith was in accordance with the Bible ; and he had successfully maintained the system against the opposition for more than a third of a century. But the circumstances surrounding him were such, at the time to which I refer, (1839–1845,) that the learned D. D. heard a different system preached from the one he had espoused ; he gave heed to it, investigated the whole subject in the light of God's word, and with an honest desire to know the truth. And the result was that he made the discovery that "sectarianism is heresy," and that he had been honestly mistaken in his theological system. He was in a fix ! Conscience said to him, *change*—be an honest man, and set yourself right.

But his pride of character, love of friends, attachment to old and long tried church arrangements, social institutions, and modes of worship, all appealed to him to hold on to the system of his fathers—"to stick to it for life." Said he to me one day, "I am now fully satisfied that you are right in the main. I have no doubt but you are right, in preaching faith as the simple belief of the truth, as revealed in the Bible. I am sure," continued he, "that you are right as to the design of baptism being 'for the remission of sins;' nothing is more clearly taught in the New Testament. And the mode, too," said he, "I have no doubt John immersed the Savior in the Jordan, and that the disciples and early Christians immersed exclusively."

Well, said I to the Doctor, if that is your faith, had you not better *change* your position, and set yourself right before God and man?

He very frankly admitted that it would be right; but said he, after a moment's reflection, "I think it hardly worth while for me to change now. It would sound so strangely to my friends. I have been preaching infant sprinkling, and practicing it, too, for more than thirty years; and during that time have sprinkled hundreds, if not thousands of babies, and if I were now, in my old age, to be immersed for the remission of sins, what would my old friends and acquaintances say of me?"

And so the learned minister did not carry out

fully the convictions of his mind ; though he did change his ecclesiastical relation, uniting with a church having more liberal views of Christianity, but not requiring immersion.

5. But we have some very eminent examples of this principle of change. Saul of Tarsus, afterwards Paul the Apostle, was a very religious man before his conversion to Christ. He tells us, that "touching the righteousness of the law, he had lived blameless." That he "had served God, in all good conscience, from his forefathers." That "he verily thought that he ought to do many things contrary to the name of Jesus of Nazareth." For many years he was entirely satisfied with his religious system, honestly believing that he was right and accepted of God.

But on his way to Damascus to persecute the Christians, he met the Lord Jesus, in the vision, and he was convinced that he was in error. Now what must he do? If you had been at Damascus in the place of Ananias, you would have said to 'him, "Stick to your system for life." Never change! But Ananias said to him, "And now, why tarriest thou? Arise, and be immersed, and wash away thy sins, calling on the name of the Lord." To this he submitted forthwith, which was an entire abandonment of his old system, with which he had been so long satisfied, and a complete change to a new system, the gospel of Christ, which he immediately preached in Damascus.

Apollos, the eloquent preacher of the baptism of John, with which he had been satisfied for years, and which he had zealously and successfully preached at Corinth, being "taught the way of the Lord more perfectly," by Aquilla and Priscilla, surrendered, and gave it up. But if you had been there, you would have advised him to change not! "Stick to it for life!"

Martin Luther was a Roman Catholic monk, and for many years fully satisfied that the system which he had honestly embraced *accorded* with the Bible. But afterwards, as you know, he was convinced by reading the Bible that he was mistaken. What was he to do now? You would have said to him, "Stick to it for life." Well, suppose he had taken your advice, and continued to maintain in the Romish Church that system which he was now fully convinced was wrong, what would have become of his honesty—of his conscience—of his manhood—of the glorious Reformation itself, which he so effectually promoted by *changing?* Did Luther do right, when he gave up his old system, and became a reformer? We all say that he acted wisely and nobly. He did just what every other man should do when he finds that he is wrong. But your advice, my dear sir, would have kept Luther and Calvin, and all the early reformers, in the old apostate hierarchy! You would have said to them: Gentlemen, I know your system is wrong, but as you have been satisfied with it, I advise you to "stick to it for life!"

6. Time would fail me to speak of John and Charles Wesley, and many other prominent men in your own church, all of whom changed. If Wesley and his colaborers in the work of developing and bringing out Methodism, had taken your advice, and "stuck to their old system for life," where would your Methodism have been to-day? Why, nowhere. It could never have been inaugurated.

But let these examples suffice. If we were all infallible, then we might talk about "sticking to it for life." But as imperfection is an attribute of our common humanity, we are liable to err, and may be honestly mistaken, and satisfied with a false system. Therefore, before your advice can be admitted as wise and safe, you must strike out *humanity*, and insert *divinity*.

7. But I will now give you what I consider the wisest and safest course for every one to

pursue. All Protestants admit that the Bible is the only infallible rule of faith and practice ; and upon the admission of all parties, human creeds and systems contain much that is erroneous—mere *trash*.

To make sure work, then, and save us from the trouble of changing afterwards, we should be very particular ; and instead of embracing a human system, supposed to accord with the Bible, let every one be certain to embrace the system taught in the Bible. To make sure of this, let him embrace the Bible, the whole Bible, and nothing but the Bible, as a system of faith and practice. He may not understand it all when he embraces it, but let him determine to study it, and to learn as much of it as he can. He may then "grow in grace and in the knowledge of the truth," as long as he lives. He may then " stick to it for life," and though he may learn many things as he advances, yet all would be in harmony with what he learned at first, and consequently he would never be under the necessity of changing. Is not this the safest course, Doctor ?

8. But the votaries of human creeds and systems are cramped in their investigations. The creed is the " iron bedstead." If found to be too short for it, they must be stretched ; and if

they grow too long, by learning more Bible truth than is in the creed, they must be *cut off* to suit the measure.

But as all these matters will come up again under your second head, I will press it no further now.

LETTER III.

Order—Government of some sort in the church is reeded—Without government, all would be confusion—Corrupt practices would creep in—What sort of government shall we have? human, or the divine?—Specific form of government—Prudential rules and regulations—God's appointment must be obeyed—The Bible the constitutional law of the church—Branches of the church, etc.

THOMAS A. MORRIS, D. D.:

My Dear Sir—We now come to the second division of your subject, which is "ORDER." This you discuss as applying to church polity and discipline. Now, in my judgment, the Apostle has no sort of reference to any thing of the kind, in the passage you quote as your text. He simply refers to the order of their worship, as a congregation of the Lord. He says: " Though absent in the flesh, yet am I with you in the spirit, joying and beholding your *order*, and the steadfastness of your faith," etc. From this passage and its context, it is evident that the Apostle is speaking of their public worship, and not of the exercise of discipline, as you seem to teach. But we shall let that pass. You commence the discussion of this branch of your subject by saying, on page 11th:

"The term order, in this connection, properly

applies to church discipline, and its administration. It will be conceded by all competent judges that government of some sort or other in the church, is requisite to her peace and prosperity. This is true of all associations, whether voluntary or involuntary. What would be the condition of your family without family government? Or of your schools without strict rules of propriety and order? Or of your State, without wholesome laws duly administered? Or of your army, without strict military discipline? And what would become of the peace, purity and prosperity of the church, without 'rules and regulations' strictly enforced? All would be in a state of anarchy and confusion, doomed to wreck and ruin, corrupt practices would creep in, confidence would be destroyed, and hatred would supersede peace and love."

In all of this, Doctor, I most heartily concur. "Order is heaven's first law." Discipline we must have in the church of God. This is a proposition that commends itself to the good sense of every right thinking person, and I think none will be inclined to dispute it. "Rules and regulations" we must have for the government of the church, or the result would be just what you describe, "anarchy and confusion." Upon this point we have no controversy with you, or any one else.

But the real issue, Doctor, is this : What sort of discipline shall we have, the *human*, or the *divine?* God has established a government in the church, and furnished it with a perfect law or discipline. Men also have made governments for the church, and manufactured disciplines for its government. So that we can now take our choice. We may choose the divine law and government, and honor God, by doing his commandments ; or we may choose the *human* discipline and government, if we like it better, and dishonor God, and ourselves by ignoring the *divine*, and adopting the *human*.

Well, Doctor, we say the divine discipline, and the divine rules and regulations, without amendment, addition or subtraction, as contained in the Holy Oracles, is the best. While you and the sects generally seem to prefer the *human!* And though you admit the correctness of our plea, by admitting the Bible to be " the only infallible rule of faith and practice ;" yet, you stultify yourself, by making what you are pleased to call your " prudential rules," for the government of your church.

We candidly believe, Doctor, that it is because the professed Christian church, or Protestant Christendom, do not adopt and live up to the divine rule, that anarchy and confusion is every where manifest. Men are not satisfied with the "divine rules and regulations," and have gone to work to improve upon them! Each party making its "prudential rules and regulations" to suit themselves, and then assuming some human name for the party, suitable to their fancy; and every day confusion becomes worse confounded! But you continue:

"We do not contend, however, that any specific form of church government is essential. The gospel is destined to prevail among all nations, and their social and political conditions are so diversified, that the same prudential rules and regulations would not be applicable to all of them. These prudential rules and regulations may, therefore, be safely varied to any needful extent, not inconsistent with the Bible, which is the constitutional law of the church generally."

Now, my dear Bishop, let us pause and calmly examine this last paragraph for a few moments. 1. You do not pretend that any "specific form of church government is essential." That is—if your words mean any thing—any *form* will do, one as well as another, if it is strictly enforced! The *human* is just as good as the *divine*, provided it is strictly enforced; no specific *form* is essential!!

Art thou a master in Israel, and knowest not

that the Lord Jesus, as King and Head of the church, has given "specific rules and regulations" for the government of his church? Will you presume to say that these are not essential? That your prudential rules and regulations will do just as well, or even better! Or do you contend that he left the law-making power entirely in the hands of uninspired men? 2. But you further say, "The gospel is destined to prevail among all nations, and their social and political conditions are so diversified that the same prudential rules and regulations would not be applicable to all of them."

This I understand to be your reason for thinking that no specific form of church government is essential. In this, however, I differ widely from you. We contend that the "specific form of church government" given to the church of Christ in the beginning, is not only "essential," but is precisely adapted to all the nations of earth. Why, sir, you might have contended with equal propriety that the gospel itself was not adapted to all nations, and therefore should be modified to suit the taste and prejudice of the people of every age and country! And some have even taken this ground! For instance:

In the beginning none but believers were baptized by the Apostles, and that was always performed by an immersion of the whole body in water, as thou very well knowest. John Calvin says, " The word *baptizo* signifies to immerse, and it is evident that immersion was the practice of the primitive church." And yet Calvin contends that the rite of baptism may be varied to suit circumstances, place, climate, etc.

In the beginning the Apostles taught believing penitents to "be immersed every one of them in the name of Jesus Christ, for the remission of sins ;" Acts ii. 38. But we are now assured by some innovators upon apostolic teaching, that though this may have been all well enough at that time, and for that people, yet in this age of progress, good manners and personal refinement, it is not to be tolerated ! It is neither polite nor fashionable now to be *immersed !* And as to remission of sins being in any way connected with baptism, the thing is an *old fogy* notion—it is "Campbellism," and not to be thought of among cultivated society and orthodox people ! The gospel must, therefore, be varied to suit the times, and to accommodate "ears polite ;" and remission of sins is now preached by "faith alone," or at the "mourner's bench ;" and thus, to keep up with the fashion of the times, Jordan is converted into a bowl ! and the sprinkling of a few drops of water upon the head of an unbelieving babe, is made to take the place of believers' immersion. Such persons no doubt think that the Abana and Parphar of their own imagination are better than the specific Jordan of God's appointment.

But you have not gone quite so far; you only contend that the specific form of church government, laid down by Christ and his inspired Apostles, is unsuitable to all nations, and may, therefore, be varied to any needful extent. To this we object. The Apostles, in their day, preached the gospel among all nations, and established churches every where; yet they did not vary the law of the Lord to suit the social and political conditions of the different nations. The specific rules and regulations laid down for the government of the church were the same every where. The Apostles had not made the important discovery that these rules and regulations were unsuited to all!

But they were a set of *old fogies*, and not at all to be compared with the theologians of this progressive and refined age. But will Bishop Morris tell us *why* these rules are unsuited to all?

4. Now, I maintain that every variation from the specific form of church government laid down in the New Testament, is a departure

from the law of the Lord, and inconsistent with the Bible, and therefore sinful. If David was right when he said, "The law of the Lord is perfect," and James, when he calls it the " perfect law of liberty," then you are grossly mistaken when you say that no form is *essential*, and that it may therefore be varied to suit the social and political conditions of those among whom it prevails! All human institutions change, and may be modified to suit circumstances, reformed and made more perfect, as human experience may require. The reason is, because human wisdom and all human systems are imperfect. But God is perfect, and whatever he does is done in divine wisdom, and therefore can never need any change or variation to make it answer the purpose for which it was intended. You are therefore radically wrong in your *assumption*.

5. But you speak of the Bible as the "constitutional law of the church generally." If I understand you, you *assume* that the different denominations, as such, are branches of the true church, and taken as a whole, they constitute what you call "the church generally."

You then make the several denominations, as branches, sustain to the Bible the same relation that the several States sustain to the Constitu-

tion of the United States. But are you right
sure, Doctor, that you are correct in this comparison? Will it hold good?

I am sure that it is a sophism. 1. The church
of Christ is a unit, and has no branch churches
or denominations. The whole figure is therefore a failure. The denominations, as such, are
not branches of Christ's church. Taken as a
whole, they do not constitute the church of
Christ. If they did, then the church would
have been imperfect till the last *branch* had
grown up! Again, if you are correct in your
figure, there would be a sort of sympathy per-
vading the whole, and a constant mutual dependence would exist throughout all the denominations. The Baptists would lean upon the
Lutherans, Presbyterians and Methodists, and
would be happy in the prosperity of all the
branches!

But is this the case? No, verily. There is
no sympathy between the Baptist and Methodist
churches, as every one knows. The Baptist denomination existed, and carried on all their op-
erations for more than a hundred years, before
the organization called the Methodist Church
had been thought of, and could continue to do
so if the Methodist Church was annihilated this
moment. This proves that they are not parts

.3

of the one great whole, but mere sects, each independent of all the others, and really in opposition to them! The branches of Christ's church are not sects or denominations, but individual members, as such. Jesus says to his disciples, not to the denominations, but to his *individual* disciples, " I am the vine, and ye are the branches."

2. But if the denominations, as such, were all branches of Christ's church, or what you call "the church generally," still your case is not made out. The Constitution of the United States fully contemplates the organization of new States, and gives them specific powers to proceed in such a work, and when organized gives such new States full power to make laws and regulations for their own government.

But the Bible does not contemplate the formation of branches or denominations, but on the contrary, strictly forbids it; and therefore it gives no authority to such branches or sects to make *"prudential rules and regulations"* for their own government! So far from it, all are required to submit implicitly to the laws of the Great King already made and published in the New Testament. You ought therefore, in justice to yourself, to abandon your sophistical figure, which has led you and thousands greatly astray.

LETTER IV.

Government of M. E. Church peculiar—Was not formed by theorizing—The result of experience and observation—A mere experiment—A human institution—Government of Christ's church no experiment—The Apostles made no experiments—The mourning bench an experiment—A mere human expedient—The Doctor brings his rules to the test—Not to the scriptural test, the word of God, but the test of experience and utility—It is the system of Methodism, and those who profess it, that we are examining.

THOMAS A. MORRIS, D. D.:

My Dear Sir—After referring to the different kinds of governments, both political and ecclesiastical, you say on page 15th: "The government of the Methodist Episcopal Church is *peculiar.* It is not entirely analogous to either of the above named systems, but does, as we think, embody the better features of them all, and exclude their objectionable ones."

Verily, Doctor, thou hast well said, that the government of your church is *peculiar!* In its government the M. E. Church is unlike any modern church; and I presume that you will no claim that it is like the government of the primitive church. It is simply "PECULIAR." But I will not anticipate.

Next, you say of your church government, "It is eminently practical; was not formed by theorizing, but is the result of experience."

The result of whose experience, Doctor? Was it the experience of the inspired Apostles of the Lamb, who were called, qualified and sent by the Master to convert the nations, and build up the church, guided by the Spirit of inspiration? This I know you do not claim. No indeed; you are too deeply versed in the Christology of the New Testament, not to know that the inspired Apostles made no *experiments* in Christianity. They taught no Methodism, or any other humanism, but spake the word of the Lord, "as the Spirit gave them utterance," and therefore made no mistakes that would afterwards be found out in the light of experience and have to be corrected.

But you evidently refer to the experience of the founders of Methodism, and their successors, the bishops and clergy of your church. And in this you are in harmony with the language of your Discipline, which we find in the address to the members, by the bishops, at the commencement of the book of Discipline. The passage runs thus:

"We believe that God's design in raising up the preachers called Methodists in America, was to reform the continent, and spread Scripture holiness over these lands. As a proof hereof, we have seen, since that time, a great and glorious work of God, from New York, through the Jersey, Pennsylvania, Delaware, Maryland, Virginia, North and South Carolina, and Georgia; as also, of late, to the extremities of the Western and Eastern States.

"We esteem it our duty and privilege most earnestly to recommend to *you*, as members of our church, our FORM OF DISCIPLINE, which has been founded on the experience of a long series of years; as also on the observations and remarks we have made on ancient and modern churches."

This address, of which the above extract is a part, is signed by the six Bishops of your church—who are : Beverly Waugh, Thomas A. Morris, Edmond S. Janes, Levi Scott, Matthew Simpson, Edward R. Ames and Osman C. Baker.

Finding your name among those appended to this address, you will not complain if I hold you responsible for the statements contained in it. According to your statement, then, both in your little book, and the Discipline, the government of the M. E. Church is a mere *experiment*, and of course a human institution. You teach us plainly that your "*form of discipline has been founded.*" Yes, "founded;" upon what is it founded, Doctor ? On Jesus Christ ? On the

Bible? No indeed, nothing of the sort. But on the *experience* of your bishops, who are all fallible men, and liable to err; and on the "observations and remarks" that you have made on ancient and modern churches. A glorious foundation for a religious system, and form of church government! The experience, observations and remarks of six men! Not inspired men, but simply Methodist preachers, who lived more than seventeen hundred years after the kingdom of Christ was set up in the world!

That I do you no injustice, is evident from another statement of yours. I quote from 15th page of your book. You say: "As Methodism arose and progressed, when the want of a rule was felt to aid the work, it was adopted. If its practical working was found to be good, it was retained; but if not good, it was modified or abolished. Thus each prudential regulation has been brought to the test of experience and practical utility, one page of which is worth more than a volume of theory."

From this we see that Methodism, according to the statement of its senior Bishop, is not only an experiment, but having no theory, it was compelled to work in the dark, and *feel* its way along, trying to supply its imaginary wants by adopting "prudential rules and regulations" of its own make, and if the *experiment* was satisfactory, retaining them; and if unsatisfactory, modifying or abolishing them altogether, and trying something else which might seem to suit better; and subjecting this again, in turn, to the same test, *experience!*

The founders of Methodism did not, and their successors in office do not know, when they adopt a rule or regulation, that it is the thing they need, or that it will answer the purpose for which it is designed; but feeling the need of something, they adopt it as an experiment, knowing that it can be changed or abolished, if it should not work up to the expectations of its friends.

By your own showing, Doctor, you have been experimenting for seventy years! During which time you have brought Methodism, which was very imperfect at first, up to its present state of perfection and prosperity. But you do not even now claim that the system of Methodism is perfect. But you speak of other changes in its polity soon likely to be made. From your own testimony, then, we must believe that the system of Methodism, as contained in your Discipline, and contended for by you, is an *imperfect, human institution*—a mere experiment. How then, Doctor, can you believe that it will "reform the continent and spread scriptural holiness over these lands ?"

Not so the church of Christ. Its government and FORM OF DISCIPLINE was no experiment. The Lord Jesus commissioned his Apostles, and gave them a divine theory, and sent them another comforter, the Holy Spirit, to guide them into all truth. According to this divine theory they worked, under the direction of the Holy Spirit, in proclaiming the glad tidings of salvation, and building up the church of Christ in the beginning.

They *felt* no need of any "rule" to "aid them in the work" of converting the nations, and therefore never adopted any by guess ! Peter says, "According as his divine power hath given unto us all things that pertain to life and godliness." If Peter was right in saying that God had given to him and his fellow disciples all things that pertained to life and godliness, it is evident that they could need nothing more to "aid them in the work."

Let us now hear Paul's testimony upon this point. Paul, stand up. You are the Apostle to the Gentiles, and preached the gospel very extensively throughout the civilized world during the first century of the Christian age. Am I right ?

PAUL.—" From Jerusalem and round unto Illyricum, I have fully preached the gospel of Christ."

Did you ever *feel* the need of a *rule* or any thing else, that you had not, to aid you in the work ?

PAUL.—"All scripture given by inspiration of God is profitable for doctrine, for reproof, for correction, for instruction in righteousness, that the man of God may be perfect, thoroughly furnished to all good works."

That will do, Paul.

All the " rules and regulations " that were necessary to make the man of God perfect, and thoroughly furnish him to all good works, Paul and Peter and their fellow-laborers found in the holy Scriptures, and of course they had no need to draw upon their own experience and observations for " prudential rules." They already possessed every thing that was necessary for the work, and therefore they never *felt* the need of any thing more, to aid them in the work of the Lord.

Now it occurs to me, Dr. Morris, that if you or your co-laborers are engaged in a work, in the progress of which you occasionally "*feel* the need of a rule to aid you in the work," that God has not furnished his church, in the holy

Scriptures, you have great reason to believe that your work is not of God, but of man ! Do you say that all your prudential rules are taken from the Bible ? I presume you will not, because if they were found there, you would not dare to "modify or abolish them." But your system being *peculiar*, "feels the need" of other rules and regulations than those furnished by inspiration ! There being no such thing as Methodism in the days of the Apostles, they made no rules for its government, and consequently it has to make rules for its own government, adapted to its many peculiarities, and in this way supply its own wants, as experience and observation seem to require !

Was it not upon this principle of *experimenting*, that you instituted the "mourning bench," or "anxious seat," for the purpose of praying penitent sinners into Christ ? I believe that Methodism claims the honor of first introducing it. You were unwilling to preach "baptism for the remission of sins," as the Apostles did in the beginning, and therefore you *"felt* the need of something to aid you in the work," and to supply this need, you adopted the "mourning bench," as an *experiment !* Its practical working was satisfactory, and you have therefore retained it, as a part of your ecclesiastical machinery! Other parties, too, seeing your success in the use of it, have adopted it also, and thus the primitive gospel has been set aside and made void by a mere human *expedient!*

But you do not claim divine authority for your "prudential rules." You inform us that all your prudential rules and regulations are brought to the "*test.*" Very well, that is right, provided always that you bring them to the infallible *test.* Paul says, "Prove all things; hold fast that which is good." But permit me to ask you, in all kindness, Doctor, to what "test" you bring your rules? To the divine law, or word of God? Nothing of the kind! You say, "Thus each prudential regulation has been brought to the test of experience and practical utility."

From this frank avowal, we see that the *"test"* to which you bring your rules is not the word of God, but your own experience! Thus the law of the Great King is lost sight of, and in its stead *human experience* is erected into a *test*—a standard, by which you determine the utility of your rules and regulations.

Considering your peculiar system of Methodism, as an EXPERIMENT—a mere human institution, (and if I understand you, you claim nothing more for it,) this may all be well enough. Viewed from such a standpoint, your system of church polity, wrought out in the work-shop of human experience and observation, is admirable, and commands the respect and admiration of the world!   Let me not, however, be misunderstood.   I am dealing with Methodism, as set forth and defended by its friends and leading men.   I am saying nothing against the members of the M. E. Church, as men.   It is the system, and not those who embrace it, that I am examining at present.

I am happy to believe that there are in the Methodist Church many good and deeply pious men and women ; among whom I number many warm personal friends ; and I would not say a word in disparagement of any of them.   Yet, believing as I do, that the peculiar system of Methodism is a *human* institution, upon the admission of its greatest men, I can not do less, as an honest man, "than speak that I do know, and testify that I have seen."   In our next we shall examine your "starting point."

LETTER V.

The starting point—The love of God—Not peculiar to
Methodism—Call to the ministry—No Methodism in
the days of the Apostles—The Apostles proved their
divine call by miracles—Modern pretenders to such
call fail to prove it—Success not sufficient proof—Personal application of redemption—Total depravity—
Conversion without outward means—Paul examined
as a witness, by Bishop Morris.

THOMAS A. MORRIS, D. D.:

My Dear Sir—I now come to your "starting
point," on the 16th page of your little book.
If I understand you, it is your object to give us
a "rapid outline view of the essential parts of
your system, and its practical workings." To
do this, you take us to your "starting point."
By which I understand you to mean the manner of starting a Methodist church. You say,
"In Methodism the starting point is, the love of
God as developed in redemption, in the gift of
the Spirit, and the divine call to the work of the
ministry. Without redemption there is no possible salvation for sinners; without the Holy
Spirit there could be no personal application of
the benefits of redemption; and without some
one be called to teach us, we should remain ignorant of our blood-bought privileges, as Paul
to the Romans, 'For whosoever shall call upon

the name of the Lord shall be saved. How then shall they call on him in whom they have not believed ? and how shall they believe in him of whom they have not heard ? and how shall they hear without a preacher ? and how shall they preach except they be sent ?' "

Well, this is rather a pretty start. Let us pause awhile and examine it. The love of God, as developed in the gift and death of his Son, is the "starting point" in Christianity ; and therefore, is not peculiar to Methodism. Christianity started seventeen centuries before Methodism was instituted, and consequently you have no right, Doctor, to claim it as the "starting point" in Methodism.

The gift of the Spirit was received on the day of Pentecost, with his miraculous gifts and powers, and was promised as a comforter and witness to all obedient believers, and is peculiar to Christianity, and you ought not to claim it as a peculiarity of Methodism. Every disciple of Christ, who has lived since the day of Pentecost, has enjoyed the Holy Spirit, before as well as after the inauguration of Methodism by John Wesley, its father. And of course it is not a peculiarity of your *peculiar* system.

As to the "divine call to the work of the ministry," I remark, that if you mean by this

·that the Apostles of the Lamb were divinely called, qualified and sent to preach the gospel to ·the nations, then I have no objection to the statement ; but I protest against your making it a peculiarity of Methodism, or the "starting point" in the formation of a Methodist church. There was no such organism as the M. E. Church in the days of the Apostles.

But if you mean that Methodist preachers are divinely called, qualified and sent, as the Apostles were, then I must be permitted to withhold my assent till I see the proof. Now, we understand you and your preachers to claim this. But I know that you can never make good this extravagant claim. And if you can not start a Methodist church until your preachers can prove their divine call to the ministry, as the Apostles proved theirs, I am sure you would ·never be able to start it !

The Apostles being immersed in the Holy Spirit, could speak in languages which they had not learned ; and they demonstrated their divine call by "signs and wonders, and divers miracles and gifts of the Holy Spirit," according to the will of God. Not so with Methodist preachers, and others who claim to be "called, qualified and sent" by the Holy Spirit. If we believe them, it must be upon their own mere as·

sertion, and without a particle of legitimate evidence. Who is prepared for this?

But even this extravagant claim is not peculiar to Methodism. Other parties made the same pretensions long before Methodism was born. Among the warring sects and parties who claim to be divinely called, qualified and sent, we find "all sorts of doctrines, preached by all sorts of men." How shall we decide who are really the called and sent? They all claim it, but none of them can furnish any proof.

One man when he rises to preach the peculiar dogmas of his sect, tells us that God has called and sent him to preach, and that he will hand it out to us just as God gives it to him! He then proceeds to give us a dish of high-toned Calvinism. Another rises on the following Lord's day, and after making similar pretensions, proceeds to warn us against the errors of Calvinsm, and, in opposition to what the first preacher taught, he proceeds to give us a sermon on Arminianism. A third gets up, and after thanking God that he has no *"larnin,"* he assures us that God has called, qualified and sent him to preach the gospel to every *"critter upon the whole living yearth,"* and proceeds to give us the peculiar dogmas of his little sect. Now, no one can believe that they are all called of God,

and sent to preach the absurdities of their re-
spective systems, as they contradict each other
most flatly ; and as they can give no evidence
of their CALL, I think the only safe course is to
reject them all, as pretenders, and cleave to the
old preachers, who were able and did establish
their divine call, beyond the possibility of a rea-
sonable doubt.

But perhaps you will say, as some of your
preachers have said, that your divine call to the
ministry of the Methodist Church is proved beyond doubt by the success that has attended
your ministry. That you have had great success in preaching the peculiarities of Methodism,
is admitted ; but the Roman Catholics have been
equally successful in preaching their heretical
doctrines, both in Europe and America, and
much more successful in her missions to China,
Japan, and other foreign countries.

Mahomet and his followers have had great
success in spreading their false religion, and
none have been more signally successful than
Joe Smith and Brigham Young, the Mormon
pretenders. If success is evidence of a divine
call, then they all have it. Yet you and I both
reject such evidence in favor of Catholicism,
Mormonism and Islamism. And if success will
not prove the divine call of the advocates of

4

these heresies, it can never prove the divinity of
your call.

The Lord commends a certain church, saying, "Thou hast tried them who say they are
apostles and are not, and hast found them liars."
But I am satisfied that God has called every
Christian to work in his great vineyard, and to
say, "*come*," according to his ability; not by a
dream, or a vague impression, but by his word.
And the very best evidence that a minister can
give that he is divinely called to the work, is,
that he PREACHES THE WORD as it was preached
in the beginning—at the "starting point" at
Jerusalem.

But we affirm that God never called any man
to preach Methodism, Presbyterianism, Baptistism, Campbellism, or any other *humanism.* The
command of Christ to his disciples was, " Go,
preach the gospel to every creature." And
John says, " They that are of God hear us [the
Apostles], and they that are not of God, hear
not us; by this we know the Spirit of truth, and
the spirit of error." Here, then, is a divine
test, by which every man's pretensions to a divine call may be brought.

But you say, " Without redemption, there is
no possible salvation for sinners; without the
Holy Spirit there could be no personal application of the benefits of redemption."

No one, Doctor, I presume, will be inclined to dispute with you as to the necessity of redemption ; but as to the *personal application* of the benefits of redemption, by the Holy Spirit, there may be some controversy. I may not comprehend your meaning, when you speak of *personal application*, but I suppose you mean about this : The sinner being totally depraved, is wholly unable to believe the gospel, repent of his sins, or do any thing else in the way of obedience to Christ ; and therefore the gospel preached to such sinners could not benefit them, or any one of them, until the Holy Spirit makes a direct personal application of the benefits of redemption, and thus enable them to believe, repent and turn to the Lord. And this is never done to whole congregations at once, but one here and another there, in the congregation, are thus personally operated on, and converted to God ; while the rest of the congregation are passed by, at least for the present, and left in a state of unbelief and sin, without the possibility of salvation, till the Holy Spirit shall come at some future time, and make a *personal application* to them, or some of them, also. Though Christ has died for them all, yet his death can avail them nothing without the "personal application."

To this monstrous dogma I object. 1st. Because the Bible nowhere teaches that all men are thus *totally* depraved. All men are more or less depraved, and some men are no doubt *totally depraved*, and "given over to hardness of heart and reprobacy of mind, that they may believe a lie and be damned." But some men are certainly worse than others, which could not be true if all men were alike totally depraved. One who is totally depraved can get no worse, for the devil is only totally depraved ; yet Paul says that "wicked men and seducers will wax worse and worse, deceiving and being deceived." Hence we see that this dogma, as held by the M. E. Church, and others, and which involves the idea of a "personal application," is false, as it is unreasonable and unscriptural.

2d. Because it destroys man's accountability to God for his actions. For if the sinner can not believe God until the Holy Spirit operates upon his heart, immediately and personally, then while he is waiting for this personal application his unbelief and disobedience can not be charged upon him as a sin, seeing that it is no fault of his. He is ready and anxious to enjoy redemption, but can not, without the personal application of it to him by the Holy Spirit, and he is waiting for that, and can do nothing to superinduce it. Therefore, his standing all the day idle is no sin.

3d. Because such a view of God's system of justification strikes down the difference between virtue and vice, righteousness and unrighteousness, and makes God the author of sin ; as he withholds the Holy Spirit from the sinner, by the direct personal agency of which he can alone obtain the ability to work righteousness.

4th. Because it makes God "a respecter of persons." According to the dogma, he makes a personal application to some and withholds it from others. Yet Peter says, "Now I perceive of a truth, that God is no respecter of persons."

5th. Because it impeaches the Divine justice. For if God sends his Spirit to make a "personal application" of the benefits of redemption to some, while he withholds it from others, how can his justice be vindicated in the damnation of those who never had the ability to come to Christ, and no personal application was made to them ?

6th. Because it contradicts the Lord's word. It makes the *personal application*, by the Holy Spirit, the power of God unto salvation. But Paul says, "I am not ashamed of the gospel of Christ, for it is the power of God unto salvation to every one that believes." Here is an irreconcilable contradiction between your system and Paul.

Again the Apostle says, "It pleased God by the foolishness of preaching to save them who believe." But your dogma contradicts the Apostle, and substitutes the "personal application" for the gospel of Christ.

I understand that when the Spirit came, at the "starting point" not of Methodism, but the church of Jesus Christ, he "convinced the world of sin, of righteousness and of judgment," and that he still does the same work, in the same way, not by immediate personal application, or by impact, but through the instrumentality of the gospel. And hence, where the gospel is not preached, no one is converted to Christ; and where the truth is not known, no one is "sanctified through the truth."

But on page 17th you proceed thus: "Now suppose a nation in which there is not one experimental, practical Christian, how would the saving knowledge of the truth first be communicated? To convert souls is God's work, but he usually employs human instrumentality to teach them their lost condition and the remedy. We say usually, but not necessarily, for he can work with or without outward means."

Yes, Doctor, God has the power to work

without means in the conversion of sinners, but does he do it? Did he ever do it in a single instance? or has he promised to do it under any circumstances? Now, so far as we can recollect, we have no example on record where any one was ever converted to God without "outward means." And the history of the church of Christ for eighteen centuries does not furnish us a single example of such conversion. By what authority, then, do you say that he "works with or without outward means" in converting men? Let us now look at a few examples of conversion, from the New Testament, and we shall see that God always employed what you are pleased to call "outward means."

When God undertook to convert the first Gentile that was converted to God, he employed "outward means." He sent an angel to Cornelius, not to tell him what he must do to be saved, but to tell him where he could get the information. "Send to Joppa for Simon Peter, and he shall tell thee words, whereby thee and thy house shall be saved." God could have converted Cornelius by a miracle, but he did not do it. He could have authorized the angel to have taught him his duty, but he did not do it, as he had not commissioned angels to preach the gospel. But Peter, the Apostle, must be sent for, who had the keys of the kingdom of heaven committed to him by the Savior, that the saving word might be heard from his mouth. You know the result.

When the Lord desired to make an Apostle of the wicked Saul of Tarsus, he appeared to him by the way, but did not tell him what he must do, as this was not his plan of saving men, but he sent him into the city of Damascus, to hear the saving word from the mouth of the disciple Ananias.

When he would introduce the gospel into Ethiopia, by the conversion of the eunuch, who was the high treasurer of the kingdom, he did not work without outward means, but sent Philip to "preach Jesus" to him. And the apostle Paul was commissioned to "go to the Gentiles, to open their eyes, and turn them from darkness to light and from the power of Satan to God." But let us put the apostle Paul upon the witness' stand again, for a few moments; and you shall have the pleasure of asking such questions as you choose. You know that he understands the matter well, and will give us definite answers.

BISHOP MORRIS—Bro. Paul, permit me to ask you a few questions upon a matter about which Bro. Mathes and I differ widely. We have agreed to leave the matter to you, as we both have confidence in your ability to answer correctly. Will you be so kind, then, as to inform us whether, in your day, God converted men with or without means?

APOSTLE PAUL—"I am not ashamed of the gospel of Christ, for it is the power of God unto salvation to every one who believes."

BISHOP MORRIS—I agree with you, Bro. Paul, that such is God's ordinary method of saving men, but have you not known many persons converted and saved by the immediate and personal operation of the Spirit, without the gospel or any other outward means?

APOSTLE PAUL—" It pleased God by the foolishness of preaching to save them that believe."

BISHOP MORRIS—Perhaps you are right in this, Bro. Paul, but I hope you will be a little more definite. Say then, if you please, have you not known persons receive faith by the *direct* operation of the Spirit, without the word of God?

APOSTLE PAUL—"So then faith cometh by hearing, and hearing by the word of God."

BISHOP MORRIS—Bro. Paul, you seem not to fully understand my meaning. I will therefore try to be a little more definite in my questions. I will ask you, then, if in your travels in heathen lands you have not now and then met with faithful, praying Christians, who had never seen a preacher, nor heard the word in any way?

APOSTLE PAUL—"How then shall they call on him in whom they have not believed? And how shall they believe in him of whom they have not heard? And how shall they hear without a preacher? And how shall they preach except they be sent?"

BISHOP MORRIS—Why, Bro. Paul, you surprise me! I have accused Bro. Mathes here of being a Campbellite, and you agree with him precisely. Indeed, Bro. Paul, if you were not the "apostle Paul," I should say that you were a "Campbellite."

LETTER VI.

The little organization—What code shall they adopt—
Let God do his own work—The contrast between the
Jerusalem church and the "little organization"—
Simple code based on the Bible—The Bible itself a
perfect code—"Little organization" must agree on
standards of faith—The standard of faith of the
church of Christ was established in the beginning—
Must be born again—The name Christian—Unconverted persons are received into the M. E. Church—
Infant church membership—Infants not allowed to
come to the Lord's table—The "capital hit."

THOMAS A. MORRIS, D. D.:

My Dear Sir—I now come to your "LITTLE
ORGANIZATION." On the 19th page of your little
book, you suppose the case of a number of persons converted in a nation where, previously,
there was no church, these being the first fruits
of the nation to God. The number of converts
making it necessary that they should be organized into a church, (Methodist Episcopal Church,
I presume you mean.)

In such an attempt of course there must be
some form about it, and some understanding as
to the "terms of fellowship," etc. You say:
" When the converts are multiplied from units
to tens, some kind of organization becomes necessary to maintain unity and peace. They
may begin with a record of all the converted

persons proposed for membership. These form the nucleus of the church. The missionary pastor and his children in the gospel are of one heart and mind. To remain so, they must adopt some simple code based on the Bible, defining their faith and practice. They must agree on the scriptural standards of morality and godliness, to prevent future difficulty," etc.

Now let us pause a moment and look at your "LITTLE ORGANIZATION." As the *nucleus* of a Methodist Church, it may do very well, but in some respects it differs widely from the first Christian church at Jerusalem, in the beginning. And you will not consider me uncharitable for showing you, and others, the contrast. But before proceeding to do so, let me say to you, Doctor, that you have only given us the case of a "little organization," who have a missionary pastor, and of course such converts have not been gathered without "outward means."

How then would you proceed in the other case which you say may occur? You say, in a nation where there are no converted persons, "God must convert some without any outward means." Very well, suppose this be done, how must they proceed to organize? and what "code" must they adopt? They have neither missionary pastor nor Bible, nor have they ever heard of the name of Jesus. If they pray, they must "call on him in whom they have not believed." And if they have any faith, they must have "believed in him of whom they had not heard." And if they have heard, they must have "heard without a preacher."

Now if converts can be made in this way, by the *direct* personal agency of the Holy Spirit, without any outward means, and an organization effected without the gospel, without a preacher, and without any outward instrumentality, or means of grace, as you teach that it can, could not God carry on the work in the same way to any extent, till the whole nation and all other nations would be converted? If so, we might as well disband all our Bible and missionary societies at once, and let God do his own work, in his own way, without any "outward means" and without our assistance!

I will now proceed to point out some of the points of difference between your "little organization" and the church of Christ, in the beginning. This may be a work of supererogation, as you do not claim that the M. E. Church is the church of Christ, or that it is even like it. Note the following particulars, then:

1. You claim that your converts are made by the *personal application* of the benefits of re-

demption, by the immediate operation of the Spirit, either with or without "outward means."

But the converts made to Christianity in the beginning (day of Pentecost and onward) were made by the use of the means which God had ordained, namely, the GOSPEL.

2. The "simple code" adopted by your little organization, you say is "based *on* the Bible." But the simple code adopted by the church of Christ, in the beginning, was the word of God itself; and not something *based on* it. You form your own code, which is of course human, and imperfect. While the code adopted by the church of Christ is divine, and furnished them by the great Head of the church, and is the "perfect law of liberty."

3. You confess frankly that your code of laws and regulations are imperfect, and have to be modified, changed, or abolished altogether, when their practical workings are found not to be satisfactory.

But the Christian code being perfect, like its Author, always works well, and can never be modified, changed or abolished during the mediatorial reign of Christ. "If any man shall add to the words of the prophecy of this book, God shall add to him the plagues that are written in the book; and if any man shall take away from the words of the prophecy of this book, God shall take away his part out of the book of life," etc.

4. You say that your "little organization" "must define their faith," etc. But as the church of Christ adopts the "faith once delivered to the saints," and the practice ordained by Christ and his Apostles, she has no need to call a council, to fix definitions, and establish terms of fellowship, as the whole matter is clearly defined in the Lord's holy word. Jesus says, "teaching them [the baptized] to observe all things whatsoever I have commanded you."

5. You tell us that your little organization must also "agree upon standards of morality and godliness, to prevent future difficulty."

But the church of Christ, taking the Bible alone as her infallible "standard of morality and godliness," has no trouble in establishing and agreeing upon "standards of morality and godliness." Her standard was established in the beginning by the Holy Spirit, and needs no adjusting.

6. So far as you inform us, your converts are made without baptism, for you make no allusion to that holy ordinance. Not so the church of Christ. Into her communion none can enter constitutionally, without baptism. Jesus says

in the great commission : "Go teach all nations, baptizing [immersing] them into the name of the Father, and of the Son, and of the Holy Spirit." Again : "Except a man be born of water and of the Spirit, he can not enter into the kingdom of God."

Peter said to the inquiring multitude. on the day of Pentecost, which was the true beginning day, when the reign of Christ as king began : "Repent, and be baptized every one of you in the name of Jesus Christ, for the remission of sins, and you shall receive the gift of the Holy Spirit." . . . . . "Then they who gladly received the word were baptized, and the same day there were added. unto them about three thousand souls." None added without immersion.

7. The name of your "little organization" is " *Methodist Episcopal Church.*" But the church of Christ wears the name of her illustrious founder, Christ. "And the disciples were first called *Christians* at Antioch." "Then Agrippa said to Paul, Almost thou persuadest me to be a CHRISTIAN." Not a Methodist, a Baptist, a Presbyterian, or a Campbellite, but simply a CHRISTIAN. Mark the difference, Doctor. Now let us hear Peter on the name ; he says, "If any man suffer as a CHRISTIAN, let

him not be ashamed." But I think if a disciple of Christ should assume the sectarian name of Methodist, Baptist, Presbyterian, or Campbellite, and should suffer on that account, he would have great reason to be ashamed.

Once more on the name. Christ is the husband, and the church is the bride; therefore as a dutiful and chaste bride, she wears the name of her husband, and rejects all other names, as unsuited to her dignity. She is, therefore, simply called CHRISTIAN, after Christ, the glorious husband and head of the church.

8. In your church unconverted persons are received to membership. Persons who are only seeking—"desiring to flee from the wrath to come." And even disorderly persons, who have been excluded from your church for gross immorality and wickedness, can turn round immediately and join your church again, on probation, without confessing the wrongs for which they were expelled. Several examples of this kind have fallen under my own observation.

Not so the church of Christ. Jesus says, "Except ye be *converted*, and become as little children, ye shall in no case enter into the kingdom of heaven." Again, "Except a man be born again, he can not see the kingdom of God." And Peter says, "Repent and be converted,

5

every one of you, that your sins may be blotted out, when the times of refreshing shall come from the presence of the Lord."

The prophet Jeremiah, in speaking of the church of Christ under the new covenant, says : "And it shall come to pass that every man shall not teach his neighbor, and every man his brother, saying, Know the Lord ; for all shall know me, from the least of them to the greatest of them." Every member of Christ's church must "know the Lord." Not an unconverted man or woman, nor an unconscious babe, in the church.

It was not so in the Jewish church, nor is it so in the M. E. Church, and many other modern religious bodies. Infants born of Jewish parents were in the Jewish church by *natural* birth—a birth of flesh and blood. Being "born after the flesh," they were entitled to circumcision on the eighth day, not to make them members of the Jewish church, but because they were members. And all such have to be "taught to know the Lord." So also it is in your church, Doctor ; the condition of membership as to infants is, " to be born after the flesh," one or both parents being members. If I understand you, infants are not sprinkled by your ministry to bring them into your church, but because they are already in it, upon the above condition. This being so, you have many thousands in your church who are recognized as members in some sense, who do not "know the Lord," and whom you must teach, "saying, Know the Lord."

9. In the M. E. Church, thousands who are recognized as members in some sense, are not permitted to come to the Lord's table. But in the church of Christ all are not only permitted to come to the Lord's table, but commanded to do so. Jesus says to them all, "Do this in remembrance of me."

Let these nine points of difference suffice for the present. Other points of comparison will come up, as we progress in our review.

On page 22d you discuss the "terms of membership in the M. E. Church." You say: "Our fathers, who gave us the outline of our present system of Methodist discipline, made a capital hit when they adopted the rule requiring a probation of at least six months prior to regular membership, a rule still enforced in all cases, except such as bring letters of recommendation from orthodox sister churches as worthy members. The condition of admission on trial is, 'a desire to flee from the wrath to come, and to be saved from sin.'"

You have well named this a "hit," and you
think it a "capital hit." It has worked well,
and you have retained it, not because it was of
God, but of the fathers, and its practical working satisfactory. You do not claim divine authority for this *hit*, but give the fathers of Meth
odism all the credit of its discovery. The Bible
furnishes no sort of countenance to it. John
Wesley made the "hit." He guessed at it, and
made the hit, and it has proved that Mr. Wesley was a good judge of human nature. It was
indeed "a capital hit!"

I need not tell one of your experience and
Scripture knowledge, that there was no such arrangement, or *hit*, in the church of Christ, in
the beginning. None were received into her
fellowship but those who were converted and
saved from their sins. None were received on
six months' trial! All who were received at all,
were taken into full fellowship and were expected to "continue steadfast in the Apostles' doctrine, in fellowship, in breaking of bread, and in
the prayers." Is it not wonderful, Dr. Morris,
that the Apostles, under the inspiration and
guidance of the Holy Spirit, did not make this
"*capital hit?*" of six months' probation, in order to membership in the church. If they had
made the hit, we should no doubt have some ac-

count of it in the following cases, where persons joined the church, who did not bring letters of commendation from other orthodox sister churches.

When Saul of Tarsus was converted, he went up into the city of Damascus and immediately commenced preaching the glorious gospel of Christ. No six months' probation in his case; he was fully converted, and a full member the very first day.

The three thousand that were immersed on the day of Pentecost, and added to them, were not probationers, on six months' trial; but were taken into full membership that very day. In proof of this we are told by Luke that "they continued steadfastly in the Apostles' doctrine, and the fellowship, and in the breaking of bread, and in the prayers; and the Lord added to them daily the saved."

There never was a more favorable opportunity to make the *capital hit* than the day of Pentecost. It was the beginning day, and Jerusalem was the beginning place. The Apostles were the divinely authorized ambassadors of heaven, called, qualified and sent by Jesus himself. And in a special manner had Jesus given the "keys of the kingdom of heaven" to Peter, and said to him, "Whatsoever thou shalt loose on earth, shall be loosed in heaven ; and whatsoever thou shalt bind on earth, shall be bound in heaven." Peter stood up with the eleven, holding the keys of the kingdom of heaven, to bind and loose, and before him were three thousand believers, all anxious to "flee from the wrath to come, and to be saved from their sins." They possessed all the qualifications of probationers, according to your rules in such cases.

If Peter had understood and approved of this *capital hit* of yours, he certainly would have applied it on that occasion; and if he had, then we should have felt bound to have used it also. If he had said to the three thousand inquirers, "If you desire to flee from the wrath to come, and to be saved from your sins, you can join us on six months' trial, and if your moral deportment is right, you can then become full members, if you choose ;" then you would have some authority. But you know that he did no such thing. They said, "Men and brethren, what shall we do ?" And Peter answered and said unto them, "Repent and be baptized, [immersed,] every one of you, in the name of Jesus Christ, (*eis*) in order to the remission of sins, and you shall receive the gift of the Holy Spirit." (See Acts ii.)

Again: Cornelius and his house were con-

verted before they joined the church. Cornelius was the first Gentile converted, and if this
capital hit, which you admit your fathers made,
had been of God, we should certainly have had
an example of it in the house of Cornelius the
Gentile. But so far from it, they were baptized
in the name of Jesus Christ, and taken into full
fellowship the first day. And without introducing other examples, I affirm positively that
the law of the Lord makes no provision for taking into his church men and women on six
months' trial, as *probationers,* upon the condition of their "desiring to fleé from the wrath to
come, and to be saved from sin," or upon any
other condition. The primitive church took
into her bosom no unconverted seekers. "They
shall all know me, from the least of them to the
greatest of them."

But, "Honor to whom honor is due." You
say the "FATHERS made a *capital hit,*" etc.
Let them have the honor of it. It is of the
fathers.

LETTER VII.

Probation—Probation more fully considered—Conditions of membership on trial—Not of God, but of the fathers—It is unscriptural—It is impracticable, as a mere human expedient—It nullifies the law of the Lord—Makes void the gospel of Christ—It shuts out of the church those whom God has received—It opens the door wide for imposition—The gospel plan much more simple—The conditions of full membership—The recommendation of a leader—Baptism—It is a human institution—Inskip's testimony—Examination before the congregation—The infant members of M. E. Church can give no assurance—Sponsors—Godfathers and godmothers—No example of the baptism of a single infant in New Testament.

THOMAS A. MORRIS, D. D. :

My Dear Sir—We now come to the "condition of membership on trial," which your fathers gave you, and which you still retain. These conditions you state correctly thus : "A desire to flee from the wrath to come, and to be saved from sin."

And you tell us that this desire to become available must be evidenced in three ways : first, by doing no harm ; by avoiding evil of every kind, etc. Secondly, by doing good, etc. Thirdly, by attending upon all the ordinances of God, etc. And you add, "If the pastor knows the candidate to come up to this standard, he can admit him at once on trial."

Now my dear Bishop, you will permit me, in
all candor and kindness, to examine this peculiarity of your very peculiar system. In my
last letter, I noticed it as an item of difference,
simply, between your church and the church of
Christ; but I wish to look more narrowly into
it, that we may understand its practical workings.

This is certainly one of your peculiarities, as
I find nothing analogous to it in any other religious system of modern times; and you do not
pretend to find an example for it in the primitive
church, or to have any divine authority for it;
for you say the fathers made it, and it was a
"capital hit." Such a thing as a "probationary membership" was wholly unknown in the
church of Christ in the beginning. The idea
seems to have originated with Mr. Wesley, the
father of Methodism. And considered as a mere
stroke of human policy, it was a *capital hit*.
But as it lays claim to no divine precept or example, we must look at it only in the light of
human reason.

As it is of the fathers, and not of God, you
will admit that we may lawfully examine it as a
mere human institution, and that we have just
as good a right to judge of it as the fathers had,
who made and adopted it, as a peculiarity of the

Methodist system, or as you have, who maintain it, as a " capital hit."

I object to the whole scheme of probationary
membership, 1st. Because it is unscriptural.
Not a shadow of a shade of evidence of any thing
of the kind can be produced from the New Testament. 2d. Because it is impracticable, even
considered as a mere human expedient. As no
one who is a mere seeker, possessing all the conditions of probationary membership—that is,
" a desire to flee from the wrath to come, and to
be saved from sin"—but who is not a Christian,
does or can "attend upon all the ordinances of
God." No Christian, enjoying the evidence of
pardon and the hope of heaven, comforted by
the Holy Spirit, can do any more than this.
Bishop Morris himself, with all his knowledge
and religious experience, can do no more than
"attend upon all the ordinances of God." How
then, Doctor, can you expect an unconverted
sinner to do it? He may when "men can ga-
ther grapes of thorns or figs of thistles !"

3d. I object to it because it sets aside the law
of the Lord, and makes void the gospel of Christ.
The law of the Lord admits all penitent believers, who " desire to flee from the wrath to come,
and to be saved from sin," to an *immediate*
union with the church of Christ, through obe-

dience to the gospel. Not as mere outside seekers, but as members of the body of Christ, and
as children of God. Witness the three thousand
on the day of Pentecost, the jailor, Lydia, Saul
of Tarsus, the Samaritans, Corinthians, and Cornelius the Gentile. It makes void the gospel of
Christ, because it tells the sinner that he need
not come now into the enjoyment of pardon and
the fellowship of the church, but may safely
wait until he has served a probation of six
months.

While all the gracious invitations of the gospel are, "now," "to-day," "Now is the accepted time," not six months hence! Dr. Morris, will you please inform us what relation your
probationers sustain to your church during their
six months of probation? You tell us they are
not members, and can not be, in the full sense
of that term, until the six months of probation
are over. Suppose the probationer should die
before his six months is out, he would die out
of your church; then what becomes of him?
If you say he would be accepted of God, and
received into glory, then you admit that your
rule upon this subject is wrong, as it shuts out
of your church those whom God accepts as his
children.

But you admit that these probationers are

sinners, and unconverted. They only "desire to flee from the wrath to come." They are not saved from their sins, but *desire* to be; how then can they be saved during their probation, if they should die? You will not say that they are saved *in* their sins. If not, they must be saved, if saved at all, by a miracle; which is unreasonable and in opposition to the teachings of the Holy Spirit.

How different to your practice was the proceedings of the inspired Apostles. When the anxious multitude inquired, "what must we do?" (see Acts ii. 37, 38,) they certain'y gave good evidence of a "desire to flee from the wrath to come, and to be saved from sin." If Bishop Morris had been in Peter's place, at that time, I suppose he would most likely have answered them in some such words as these: "Come forward to the anxious seat, and we will pray for you, and perhaps God will have mercy upon you and pardon your sins; and then you who get religion, and you who get no religion, can become probationary members of our church, for six months on trial, provided you evince 'a desire to flee from the wrath to come, and to be saved from sin,' and at the end of the six months' trial, if you still evince such a desire, we will take you into full fellowship, though you may have no religion."

But Peter and the rest of the Apostles, not understanding this "capital hit" of your fathers, admitted the whole three thousand to baptism and full membership and fellowship in the church the very same day. That they were all in fellowship, is evident from a declaration of Luke in the same chapter. Referring to those persons added on that day, he says, "And they continued steadfastly in the fellowship," etc. They were *in* "the fellowship," or they could not have *continued* in it.

4th. Once more; I object to this rule of your church, because, in my judgment, it opens wide the door for imposition; the very thing, I presume, that it was intended to guard. One of your members, perhaps a preacher, commits some grievous offense against the peace and dignity of your church. He is brought before your tribunals, and convicted of the sins charged against him. He is admonished, but refuses to repent and acknowledge the sins proved against him, but continues to deny them in the face of positive testimony, and he is therefore expelled from your church, as unworthy of your fellowship, to be to you "as a heathen man and a publican." Then, sir, there is nothing in your system to prevent such profane man from joining again the very same day on probation; provided he " evinces a desire to flee from the wrath to come, and to be saved from sin." And some have availed themselves of this rule of yours, to my certain knowledge, to the great chagrin of the members generally, but it could not be helped.

How much more simple the good old gospel plan, to admit all into full fellowship in the church immediately who believe the gospel, re-pent of their sins, confess Jesus before men, and are baptized "into the name of the Father, and of the Son, and of the Holy Spirit." And if such person sin, so as to justify the church in withdrawing her fellowship from him, he can only be restored by repentance, confession and prayer.

CONDITIONS OF FULL MEMBERSHIP.

You say, " The conditions of full member-ship after probation, are three : First, a recom-mendation of a leader, with whom the candidate has met at least six months on trial, who has every opportunity to know his religious state, daily walk, and general bearing. Secondly, he must be consecrated to God in baptism, either in infancy or adult age, this being the initiating ordinance into the visible church of Christ. Thirdly, he must on examination by the minister in charge, before the church, give satisfactory assurance both of the correctness of his faith and his willingness to observe and keep the rules of the church." And you add, "These conditions are few and simple, but indispensable; and taken altogether they show conclusively that our church is at least as well guarded against imposition in the reception of members as any other church."

If you mean to compare your church with other modern churches, which are also governed by human laws, rules and regulations, like itself, I am willing to admit the correctness of the comparison, and the conclusion you draw from it. But if by the expression, "any other church," you aim to include the primitive church, governed by the perfect law of the Lord, and those occupying the same ground now, having the same faith and practice, and governed by the same divine code of laws, and wearing the same divine name, "Christian," then I must deny your conclusion—you are not as well guarded against imposition. But I desire to make a few remarks upon your conditions of "full membership."

"The recommendation of a leader with whom the candidate has met at least six months on trial."

This first condition establishes beyond a doubt

the fact that your church is peculiar, and unlike the church of Christ. Where did the Apostles ever require such recommendation of a leader? What leaders had lived and held class meetings six months before the day of Pentecost, so that they might recommend the three thousand converts who were added to the church the same day? These converts had not been giving evidence for the previous six months that they "desired to flee from the wrath to come, and to be saved from sin;" but on the contrary, only fifty days before, many of them had participated in the murder of the Lord Jesus Christ, saying, " his blood be upon us and upon our children." Yet they "gladly received the word, and were baptized, and the same day were added to them about three thousand souls."

Your rule, or first condition of membership, would have compelled the "three thousand" to have joined on trial merely, and to have waited at least six months, in order to have procured the necessary recommendation from their class leaders, so that they might have come into the church in full fellowship, as full members! But the church of Christ had no condition requiring a probation of six months, and so they were admitted at once. With what leader had the eunuch met six months, before Philip bap-

tized him and received him into full fellowship?
None. Can you furnish me with a single example where any of the converts made to Christianity by the Apostles were required to bring
"a recommendation of a leader with whom they
had met for at least six months?" You know,
Doctor, that you can not furnish an example,
and of course you will not try; and yet you say
that "these conditions are indispensable!" Indispensable they may be to admission into your
church as full members; but the church of the
living God has no such conditions.

Your second condition is "baptism either in
infancy or adult age." But why, Doctor, do
you make baptism, either in the infant or adult,
a condition of full membership? Because you
say, it is the "initiating ordinance into the visible church of Christ."

This is a very good reason, provided the
Methodist Church is the church of Christ. But
this, as I have proved in a former letter, you do
not claim, nor does your Discipline nor any of
your prominent writers claim it. Mr. J. L. Inskip, one of your prominent authors, in his book
on Methodism, on 65th page, says of your
polity:

"A more wise or better arranged system of
religious and moral enterprise, could not have

6

been conceived. Of course, like all other human institutions, it has defects and imperfections." The reader will please note particularly the expression, in the above quotation, "*like all other human institutions.*" According, then, to this oracle of Methodism, the whole system of Methodistic polity, which you, Bishop Morris, defend and extol so highly, is a mere *human institution*, wise and well arranged.

But allow me to ask you, Bishop, if baptism be the initiating ordinance into the visible church, can any one get into it who has not been baptized? And if infants are entitled to baptism, as you claim, are they not thereby initiated into the visible church of Christ? And are they not, as a matter of course, entitled to full membership? If so—and I think you will admit the correctness of the conclusion—then what becomes of your "six months' trial," and "recommendation of a leader" with whom they must have met at least six months on trial?

And worse still; you do not even permit your infant members to "attend upon all the ordinances of God." You do not permit them to come to the Lord's table, which you will certainly admit is one of the ordinances of God, and is enjoined upon every member of Christ's body, "from the least to the greatest of them."

If the Lord's supper is an ordinance of God, and enjoined upon all the members of his church, it must be the duty of all to partake of it. If you are correct, then, in making baptism a condition of full membership, and infants have a right to it, as you say, then they become full members the moment they are baptized, and entitled to all the privileges of the church, and all the ordinances of the house of God, of which they are now full members. Whoever, then, would stand in the way and hinder these babes, (if they are initiated into the visible church by baptism, as you teach,) from partaking of the emblems of the broken body and shed blood of the Lord, are guilty of a great sin. If you admit them to baptism, you can not reject them from the Lord's table, as both go together. What answerest thou, Doctor?

Your third and last condition of full membership is, also, one for which you have neither precept nor example in the word of God. When or where did the Apostles ever examine a candidate for membership before the whole congregation, and require him to give "assurances of the correctness of his faith," and his willingness to keep and observe all the rules of the church, before they would receive him into full membership? Never! nowhere! They simply required penitent believers to confess their faith in Christ, and upon such confession they baptized them and received them into the fellowship of the church, as thou knowest very well.

Will Bishop Morris be so kind as to inform us how the infant members of his church can "give assurances of the correctness of their faith," when they have no faith, correct or incorrect?

These infants, according to your peculiar system, have been initiated into your church by baptism, and consequently are in full fellowship. But how did they, at their initiation, give you assurance of their willingness to observe and to keep all the rules and regulations of your church? They know nothing about your rules. Or will you fall back upon the old exploded notion of "sponsors," "godfathers and godmothers," to answer for the babes? I see no other chance for you. But you will admit that this was a human contrivance, and a very profane one at that. For it often happened, in time past, and even now in the Episcopal Church, and the Roman Catholic Church, that wicked and profane men and women stand and answer for the child, as "godfathers and godmothers." No, you will not contend for this.

Well, then, what will you do with the case?

Will you say that infants are not *initiated* into the church by baptism, as full members? Then you admit that infants are not scriptural subjects of baptism, and of course that you have no scriptural right to baptize them. But whatever may be your position upon this point, one thing you know, Doctor, and that is, that you can not produce a single example in the New Testament of the baptism of a single infant, or of the reception of a single infant into the church of Christ. It is a human tradition, not of God, but of the fathers.

LETTER VIII.

BILL OF RIGHTS.

Persons joining the M. E. Church acquire right—An interest in all the church property, etc.—It amounts to twenty millions of dollars—Each member's interest in church property about $2"—Deeds to church property, how made—Religion of Jesus offers no worldly inducements—All Christian privileges were fully enjoyed long before the M. E Church was organized—The class meetings—Love feasts—The Christian "feast of charity"—Infancy of Methodism, etc.

THOMAS A. MORRIS, D. D. :

My Dear Sir—We now come to the consideration of your " BILL OF RIGHTS." On the 27th page of your little book you say :

"By becoming a member of the Methodist Episcopal Church, you acquire rights which you never had before, and never could have possessed without such membership."

Have we the right to worship God, as his word and our conscience may dictate, without becoming members of the M. E. Church? We have. Has any one but a Methodist a right to pray? Yes, all true believers have a right to cry "Abba, Father." Have we the right to obey the Savior and enjoy "the love of God shed abroad in our hearts" without joining the M. E. Church? We have. Have we a right to the Spirit of adoption, without being Methodists?

We have. In a word, have we not all the rights, privileges and immunities of citizenship in the church of Jesus Christ, and access to all the means of grace that God has ordained, for our spiritual life, growth and improvement, in all that pertains to life and godliness, without becoming members of the Methodist Episcopal Church? Certainly we have; and I feel confident that you, my dear Bishop, will most cheerfully admit it. There were no Methodists in the world for some FIVE THOUSAND SEVEN HUNDRED YEARS after the creation of the world, and yet those who obeyed God were blessed and saved.

The Christian church, from the day of Pentecost till the inauguration of Methodism in the eighteenth century, enjoyed all the means of grace, and all the ordinances ordained by Jesus Christ, and as Peter expresses it, they had "all things that pertain to life and godliness." And yet they were not members of your church, as there was no such church in existence during all that period.

What wonderful "rights," then, Doctor, have you to offer in the M. E. Church that were not fully enjoyed by the primitive Christians; or that can not be enjoyed now, just as well and as completely, out of the M. E. Church, as in it? You say:

"And first, you secure an interest in all the church property, which, in houses of worship, parsonages, cemeteries, and institutions of learning, with their ground plats, amount to at least twenty millions of dollars."

Well, we must own up, I suppose, that no one has any interest in your vast church property, but the members of your church. In some neighborhoods, villages and towns, appeals have been made to the liberality of the outside community, and members of other sects, and to our brotherhood, to aid in building your houses of worship; and they have done so, under the impression that they would have some interest in them; but they have generally found out their mistake after the house was built.

You claim, I believe, to have a million of members. Then according to your statement above, each member has an acquired right to an interest in your church property to the amount of TWENTY DOLLARS! Now I ask you, in all humility, my dear Bishop, in bringing this item forward in the manner you have, does it not look a *little*, just a *little*, like offering a premium of twenty dollars in property to any one who will join your Methodist Episcopal Church? It certainly does look a little that way; but still I do not charge you with such a design.

But let us look a little after this property question.

It is not generally known, perhaps, that all your deeds for church property are so made to the M. E. Church in *general*, that if every member of the church in any particular locality were to change their religious views, and as a church without a dissenting voice should agree to take the word of God as their only guide and directory from earth to heaven, and should unanimously, class leader, preacher and all, take the name "Christian," as given by divine authority to the disciples of Christ, first at Antioch, and which was worn exclusively by them for many centuries—I say, if they should do all this unanimously, the Methodist Episcopal Church could come from other localities and take possession of their meeting house, and turn the real owners of the property, who had built the house with their own labor and money, out of doors!

Therefore, to retain this acquired right in church property, to even the twenty dollars, the initiated must continue to profess the doctrines of the M. E. Church, as set forth in the twenty-five articles of her Discipline, and conform to her peculiar rules and regulations. Thus you see, Doctor, that in your church all progress in the knowledge of the truth is defeated, and you become stereotyped in the doctrines and traditions of your fathers.

But after all, Doctor, is not this rather an appeal to denominational pride, and to love of worldly aggrandizement? Is it not, in effect, saying: We are a rich and powerful denomination. We are very numerous, and own by deed at least *twenty millions* of property. By uniting with us, as a member, you will become a partner and joint heir in this vast inheritance of the M. E. Church.

The religion of Jesus offers no inducements of a worldly nature to any one to become a Christian. The Lord himself was poor, so poor that he had not where to lay his head. And he distinctly told his disciples that they must forsake all and follow him. Their houses and lands had to be given up, yea, and their own lives also, if the cause required the sacrifice.

Paul in his preaching talked not of worldly honor, or riches; but of stripes and imprisonments, chains and dungeons, poverty and wretchedness in this world; but a crown of glory in the world to come, with everlasting life. But he never boasted of the wealth of the church, in meeting houses, cemeteries, institutions of learning, ground plats and parsonages, as an inducement to persons to join the church. He was so poor himself that he "had no certain dwelling place." And looking over the whole ground, he decided that "the love of money is the root of all evil." And the Lord said to his disciples, "Lay not up for yourselves treasures on earth." But I will press this matter no further at present, as I suppose you only mentioned your wealth incidentally, and did not really intend to offer a premium in church property to induce persons to join your church. But let us now hear the second item in your "bill of rights." You say:

"Secondly, by becoming a member of the Methodist Episcopal Church, you have acquired a full share in all her privileges. This includes an interest in her sympathies, her prayers, and her ample means of religious instruction and encouragement; in her ordinances, including the holy eucharist, and in her powerful ministry and pastoral oversight," etc.

On this point I need say but little, as you will admit that Christian sympathy, prayers, and ample means of religious instruction and encouragement, the ordinances of the house of God, including the Lord's supper, or "eucharist," as you term it, with the ministry of the word and pastoral oversight, can all be acquired and fully enjoyed out of the Methodist Church ; as all these rights and privileges were fully enjoyed by Christians for seventeen centuries before the M. E. Church had an existence ; and of course nothing of importance would be gained by joining your church, which can not be enjoyed as fully out of it.

Do not Presbyterians, Baptists, Congregationalists, and all other "evangelical sects," as you call them, enjoy all the rights and privileges which you enumerate in your "secondly?" You will admit it, I am sure ; and I think you will admit also that the Christian Church, who reject all party names, creeds and confessions of faith, of *human* manufacture, and who takes the Bible alone as her rule of faith and manners, and the name "CHRISTIAN," as the name given to the disciples of Christ in the beginning—I say, you will admit that they too enjoy all these privileges and rights as fully as Methodists, except it be in your "powerful ministry." And I am sure that you will not deny that the Christian Church has a "powerful ministry," who in point of talents, learning and piety will lose nothing in comparison with the ministry of the M. E. Church.

But you further say to your people, under this head : "You have all the privileges found in any other evangelical church, with class meetings and love feasts into the bargain, two choice means of religious improvement, at once profitable and delightful."

Now, Dr. Morris, I admit that you have brought forward something new ; and if they are what you say, "profitable and delightful," it might be well enough for every body to acquire the right of using them, by joining your church. You admit above that all the Christian privileges to be found in your church, can also be found in all other evangelical churches, except the two last named, which you tell us that the members of your church "get into the bargain ;" that is, "class meeting and love feast." Let us then look at these two means of "religious improvement," and see what they amount to.

CLASS MEETING.—Mr. Inskip in his book on Methodism, p. 193, says of the class meeting : "And so soon as we become willing to dispense with this feature of our system, our decline and downfall will certainly and rapidly follow. This is one of the ancient landmarks. And it would be almost sacrilege to remove or deface it."

From this it is evident that the class meeting is regarded of vital importance to the very existence of Methodism. And yet, my dear Bishop, Mr. Wesley knew that such an institution as a class meeting was never heard of in the primitive church. It is entirely destitute of Scripture warrant. Or will you say, as Mr. Wesley did, when he was called on for his Scripture authority for it. He answered : " There is none against it." Nor does the Scripture in so many words condemn the use of instrumental music in our worshiping assemblies ; but shall we conclude, therefore, that it is scriptural and right ? Infant sprinkling is not once named or alluded to in the Bible, and of course we find no Scripture in so many words, and by name forbidding the practice ; and Dr. Clarke regards this as a strong argument, if not the very strongest in its favor ! Class meetings are of *human device*— not of God, but of the fathers of Methodism. It may be, and no doubt is, a good *human* expedient, to keep Methodism alive, as Mr. Inskip assures us that it would starve and die without it. But the Christian church depends not upon class meetings, or any other human device, to give it success. But of "class meetings" I shall have more to say hereafter.

Love Feasts.—Your love feasts, like your class meeting policy, has no Scripture warrant, and is therefore, a mere human expedient. I believe your love feasts are generally observed at the close of your quarterly conferences, yearly conferences, and other great occasions. At such times, I believe it is your custom to issue tickets to such persons as the elders and preachers think proper to invite. These invitations, I believe, extend, not only to members of your church in good standing and full fellowship, but also to well-wishers of the cause of Methodism, though they may not be professors of religion at all ! When the hour arrives, the congregation thus brought together, sit down together, while bread and water are passed round, each one taking a bite of the bread, and a sip of the water ! This is one of the two delightful means of religious instruction, which "every Methodist gets *into the bargain,*" as you inform us ! But Doctor, do not some other sects, besides the M. E. Church, use the "love feast" and the "class meeting" too ? So it seems that these sects enjoy these "delightful means of religious instruction," without joining your church.

But you are perhaps ready to say that you have some Scripture at least, for the "*love feast,*" as the apostle Jude says of certain ungodly teachers. "They are spots in your feasts of charity ;" (Jude 12.) We have the testimony of the learned, that there was something called "feasts of charity," or "love feasts," in the primitive church, which were continued up to the fourth century.   But you will not contend that these " love feasts," or " love suppers," as Tertullian calls them, were any thing like your " love feasts."

The great Dr. Benson, one of your principal commentators, says of these ancient "love suppers."

" They were called *love feats*, or *suppers*, because the richer Christians brought in a variety of provisions to feed the poor, the fatherless, the widows, and strangers, and ate with them to show their love to them."

Now, Doctor, if you will change the character of your "love feasts," to something like the above, and make it a real feast of love, to the poor, the widow and the orphan, and the stranger, then I will cease to oppose it.   What say you ?

In giving us the third item in your "bill of rights," you say :

" Thirdly, these acquired rights are secured to you on such a firm constitutional basis, that no earthly power can deprive you of them, till you willfully forfeit them by disobedience to, or some personal · violation of, the rules of the church."

That is, your members acquire the right to stay in the M. E. Church, as long as they conform to your peculiar rules. You admit that in the "infancy of Methodism," the preacher had absolute power over the laity, and could dispossess them of all their privileges, at his pleasure, and without the form of a trial. But it was found not to be safe for the members, and the power was taken from him : and now the laymen are allowed a trial before their "peers."

Very well, Doctor, that was a good step n the path of reformation. Go on, my dear sir, reforming your peculiar system, till you have got back to primitive ground, and a "*pure speech.*" Then, indeed, all that is really peculiar to Methodism will be laid aside as useless to the Christian, and the word of God alone will take its proper place as your only guide from earth to heaven. If we take all the human systems of religion in Christendom, and examine them in the light of divine truth, we should no doubt find many truths taken from the Bible, in all of them, and a great many things *peculiar* to each. Whatever therefore is true in any of them, is not *peculiar* to them, but divine. And whatever is *peculiar* to Methodism, Baptistism, Presbyterianism, Episcopalianism, or any humanism, is not of God, but of men, and therefore not essential to salvation, and may be safely laid aside as useless lumber.

7

We must necessarily pass over much that you have said, as the limit we have set to these letters will not admit of a more extended examination.

LETTER IX.

THE MINISTRY.

Three agents standing between the pastor and his flock—Deacons—Class leaders and class meetings unknown in the beginning of Methodism—Rise of Methodism—Mr. Wesley an unconverted man for near ten years after he began to preach Methodism—Whence came class meetings?—Captain Foy the father of class meetings—It is a prudential regulation—A hard question—Exhorters and local preachers—Presiding elders—An experiment of seventy-four years' standing—The Bishop's cabinet—Better proof than age—The experiment has proved successful—Romanism has been successful—Mahomet and Joe Smith have both been successful with their delusions—We must have something better—A "thus saith the Lord"—The divine pattern of a church shown at Jerusalem.

THOMAS A. MORRIS, D. D.:

My Dear Sir—On the 38th page of your little book, you speak of the ministry of your church on this wise:

"Between the members and pastors there are other active agents for good; class leaders, exhorters and local preachers."

From your statement it appears that these three classes of agents, or ministers, stand "between the members and their pastors," and of course they are above the members. It was not so from the beginning. In the primitive church no agents were placed over the members, between them and their pastors. They had their deacons, but they were not placed over their brethren, but rather under them, as "servants" of the congregation, and by virtue of their office they performed no pastoral work. They had charge of the temporal affairs of the church, and served tables. (Acts vi.) Those of them who used the office of a deacon well, "obtained a good degree, and great boldness in the faith." And two of them, at least, became powerful preachers, as Philip and Stephen. But preaching constituted no part of their business, as deacons.

And even in the beginning of Methodism, such agents as class leaders and class meetings were wholly unknown. You are no doubt well posted in the history of your church, and of course you need not be told that at the *first* rise of the Methodist Society it consisted of only four young men, and even these were *unconverted !* They met occasionally of evenings, to read the Greek classics and converse together. This was in Oxford, England, in 1729. Mr. Wesley's own words in reference to this matter are the following :

"On Monday, May 1st, our little Society began in London ; but it may be observed, that the first rise of Methodism, so called, was in No-

vember, 1729, when four of us met together at
Oxford." And Mr. Wesley further says, "The
second rise of Methodism was at Savannah, Ga.,
in 1736, where twenty or thirty persons met at
my house." And again he says, "The third
rise of Methodism was in London, May 1, 1737,
when forty or fifty of us agreed to meet together
every Wednesday evening, in order to a free
conversation, begun and ended with singing and
prayer."— *Wesley's Works, Vol. 7, p.* 348.

Here we have the history of the rise and progress of your *peculiar* system of Methodism,
for near ten years, embracing three distinct
risings; yet there is no reference made to class
leaders, or class meetings, simply because the
thing did not then exist. And what is very remarkable in this matter, is the fact that Mr.
John Wesley, the founder and father of Methodism, was all this time an *unconverted* sinner !
According to his own testimony, he was only
converted to God on the 4th day of May, 1738,
near ten years after he commenced preaching
Methodism. (Wesley's Works, Vol. 3, p. 74.)

Whence, then, came class leaders and class
meetings ? You say this is an essential part of
your system, and is peculiar to it ; and Mr. Inskip says that it is so important to the life of
Methodism, that if it should by any means be,

laid aside, your *"decline and fall would certainly and rapidly follow."*   Yet we have
seen, from the history of Methodism, that nothing of the kind existed for some ten years after
the *first* rise of Methodism in Oxford.   But we
are not left in the dark upon this subject.   One
of your leading writers, while giving the history
of Methodism, says upon this point :

"In the month of February, in the year 1742,
several 'earnest and sensible' men, as Mr. Wesley calls them, connected with the Society under
his care at Bristol, were together consulting as
to the best method to be adopted to secure the
payment of a debt incurred in building a 'preaching place.'   It was agreed that the Society be
divided into classes of twelve, and that one of
them should be appointed to collect of each of
these what they might be willing to give.   The
same arrangement was made in London, about a
month after."—*Inskip, p.* 192.

But Mr. Wesley himself is a little more definite in his history of this matter.   Speaking of
this Bristol conference of "earnest and sensible
men," he says :

"I asked, how shall we pay the debt upon
the preaching house?   Captain Foy stood up
and said, 'Let every one give a penny a week,
and it will easily be done.'   'But many of them,'

said one, 'have not a penny to give.' 'True,' said the Captain, 'then put ten or twelve of them to me. Let each of them give what they can weekly, and I will supply what is wanting.' Many others made the same offer." So Mr. Wesley divided the Society among them, assigning a class of about twelve persons to each of these, who were termed "leaders." (Wesley's Works, Vol. 7, p. 316.)

Here, then, we have found the origin of class meetings and class leaders, in the goodly town of Bristol, in "merry old England," in the year of grace 1742, just thirteen years after the "first rise of Methodism." This institution originated in the prolific brain of Captain Foy, who seems to have been a good financier, and as a stroke of financial policy he certainly made a "capital hit."

But let it be observed, that the design of the institution at first was not to place "class leaders" over the members to perform pastoral duties, between the pastor and his flock, which you inform us is the position now occupied by such functionaries in your church; but it was simply an arrangement suggested and set on foot by the good Captain Foy, for the purpose of raising the money necessary to pay the debt on the meeting house, and of course temporary in its character and design.

Such, my dear Doctor, is a brief, but true history of the rise of class meetings and class leaders, by which you and all our readers will see that it is not from heaven, but of men. Class leaders are an order of officials wholly un-known in the primitive church, and of course entirely unnecessary to the growth and prosper-ity of the Christian church, and to the salvation of man. But Mr. Inskip says of this peculiar institution :

" Class meetings are peculiar to Methodism. Other churches have occasional inquiry, confer-ence, or experience meetings; but the class meetings are an ESSENTIAL PART OF THE SYSTEM. All persons uniting with us, are required to at-tend class, unless prevented by sickness or other circumstances not under their control. It is not claimed that this institution is of divine ori-gin. Like many other peculiarities of our sys-tem, it is a prudential regulation." . . . . "And so soon as we become willing to dispense with this feature of our system, our decline and downfall will certainly and rapidly follow."—*Inskip's Methodism, pp.* 192–3.

Now, my dear Bishop, what respect can we entertain for a religious system which depends for its very existence upon a mere *humanism*— " a prudential regulation," for which no "divine authority" is claimed, even by its most ardent advocates and supporters ? Can such a system be of God ? You need not attempt to answer this question, if you think it is too hard for you, and your silence will be understood by all. In-deed, I do not expect you to answer it.

But let no one misunderstand me, while I thus speak of the " peculiarities of Methodism." It is the system, and not those who honestly embrace it, that I am opposing. I know that the system is wrong, and therefore I oppose it with earnestness, and use great plainness of speech ; though I have great respect for you, Doctor, and all other good Methodists. I have no doubt that many Methodists are sincere and pious ; and it is because I love you and them, that I speak thus plainly of your system. And may I not hope that you will not consider me " your enemy because I tell you the truth ?"

As to your other two agents, "exhorters and local preachers," so far as they are peculiar to Methodism, and come between the pastor and his flock, and are above the members, the same remarks and objections that we have already made concerning class meetings and class leaders will apply in all their force.

It is true there were exhorters in the primi-tive church, but they were not an " order of men," above the church. Every member was authorized to exhort his brethren. "Exhorting one another, and so much the more as you see the day approaching." But they were not officers, licensed by the preacher in charge, or the quarterly conference; nor were they placed above their brethren, " between the members and the pastor."

The early Christians appear to have been nearly all preachers, not *local*, but itinerant preachers. We are told, Acts viii. 1–4, that when Stephen was put to death, "there was a great persecution against the church which was at Jerusalem, and they were all scattered abroad throughout the regions of Judea and Samaria, except the Apostles." . . . . "Therefore they who were scattered abroad, went every where preaching the word."

Thus we see that they were all scattered abroad; and that all who were thus dispersed, "went every where preaching the word." The Apostles remained in Jerusalem, and were, at least for the time being, the only " local preachers" among them. And their commission was to "every creature." Every one was required to do all he could for the advancement of the cause of Christ. Jesus says, "Occupy till I come." Whether the Christian had one, two, or five talents, he was required to improve them according to his ability. But such an order of men as " local preachers," being placed above their brethren and between the members and their pastors, was never thought of among the primitive disciples.

PRESIDING ELDERS.

On page 5th you say of the office of "presiding elder :''

" The office first appears on the minutes of 1785, where an elder's name stands at the head of each district, but without the prefix 'presiding' till 1789, just seventy years ago, since which period the minutes in this respect have been uniform. A usage of seventy-four years' standing is entitled to respectful consideration. It has, however, higher claims than age confers, on the score of utility. The experiment has proved itself successful.''

Well, Bishop, that will do. The office of presiding elder, according to your own showing, is an *experiment* of only seventy-four years' standing. Such an officer was not only unknown in the Methodist Church during the first half century of its existence, but had no existence in the Christian church for seventeen centuries, and is never referred to in the New Testament! Some seventy-five years ago your fathers "felt the

need" of something to come in between the itin-
erancy and the bishops, for the purpose of form-
ing the "BISHOP'S CABINET." And not knowing exactly what they did want, they created the
office of "Elder" to stand at the head of each
district, but finding by experiment that this was
not exactly what they needed, they placed the
prefix "presiding" to the "elder," four years
afterwards, and the *experiment* then worked
well, and it has been retained as part of the system.

But you say you have better evidence in its
favor than age (seventy-four years). Well,
Doctor, let us have it ; we want something better than that, before we are prepared to admit its
divine authority. Christianity is more than
eighteen hundred years old, and this part of your
peculiar system can only be traced back some
seventy-five years, and can consequently claim
nothing on the score of antiquity. But let us
have your best and strongest proof.

You say, "The experiment has proved itself
successful." And is this the best you can do,
Doctor, for your "presiding elder ?" I suppose it is, and will therefore examine it for a moment. Did it never occur to you, my dear
Bishop, that this argument would prove too
much for your purpose ? Has not the Romish

Church been very successful in the use of the mass, the confessional, penance, and purgatory? You know that she has been very successful in the use of these unscriptural and miserable dogmas. Abolish any or all of these, and her "decline and downfall would certainly and rapidly follow." But does the argument of success prove Romanism to be from God? Certainly not.

Mohammed was very successful in promulgating the Koran. But did his success prove his system right, and his religion acceptable to God? What say you?

Joe Smith, the modern pretender, was very successful in the promulgation of the "Book of Mormon." You know that unprecedented success attended the efforts of Smith and his deluded followers in establishing their miserable delusion; but so far from receiving this success as evidence of the divinity of Mormonism, you and I regard the system and the practice under it as an abomination in the sight of God, and that their success only proves the *gullibility* of the people. Is this not so, Doctor?

No indeed—we Protestants want better evidence for any doctrine, practice, or office in the church, than mere success, or utility. We must have a "thus saith the Lord." And therefore any office, doctrine, or practice, that does not date back more than seventy-five years we reject as having no authority that we are bound to respect; and wanting in all the essential elements of a Christian institution.

You remember that God said to Moses, when he was about to make the tabernacle, "See that thou make all things according to the pattern shown thee in the mount." This tabernacle was a type of the Christian temple, or church of Christ. God has shown us the pattern of the "church of the living God." This divine pattern was the church constituted at Jerusalem, on the day of Pentecost, when the Holy Spirit came down, according to the promise of Jesus, and "guided them into all truth."

To this model we must always refer; and if we should find that in our honest efforts to build up the church of Christ, and "spread scriptural holiness over these lands," we have made a mistake, and have entirely failed to "make all things according to the divine model or pattern" shown us at Jerusalem, and that instead of "spreading scriptural holiness over these lands," we have been building up a sect of very recent date, and spreading Methodism, Presbyterianism, or Campbellism "over these lands;" I say, if we find that we have been thus engaged, no matter how honestly, we ought at once to acknowledge our errors, reform and set ourselves right.

For example, if we should find from an examination of the "divine pattern," as given to us in the New Testament, that in the Jerusalem church, and those organized under the eye of the Apostles, there were no "class meetings," "class leaders," "local preachers and exhorters," such as we find in the M. E. Church, placed over the congregation and between the members and the pastor, no "presiding elders" over the traveling preachers and between them and the bishops, to form the "Bishop's cabinet," we should then be satisfied at once that we have not "made all things" according to the "pattern shown us" in the mount of God; and we should at once give these things all up, and abandon them as an *excrescence* upon the tree of life.

Or if we should find in our examination of the "pattern," that none were received into the primitive church without faith in Christ, as the Son of God, repentance, confession of Jesus Christ, before men, as the Savior of sinners, and immersion in the name of Jesus Christ, *into* the name of the Father, and of the Son, and of the Holy Spirit; and that this immersion was for, or in order to, or *into* the "rémission of sins," we could then apply the divine pattern to our work, and see whether we have been working according to it.

And if we find that we have been working and "experimenting" upon rules and regulations of our own make, for a hundred years, under which we have taken into our church unconverted persons and infants without faith ; and that we have changed immersion into the unmeaning rite of *sprinkling* or *pouring*, then we may know with absolute certainty that we are wrong, however sincere we may have been in our efforts.   .

And on the other hand, if in our examination of the divine pattern, we find that we have the same faith, the same divine regulations for receiving members into the church, and of withdrawing fellowship from unruly members ; that we have the same immersion, and submit to it with the same design ; that we wear the same name, speak the same things, and mind the same things ; then we may know certainly that *we are right, and can not be wrong.*

LETTER X.

THE BISHOPS.

New Testament bishops compared with Methodist bishops—*Episkopoi* means " overseers"—A plurality of overseers in every congregation—Methodist bishops have no local diocese—Primitive overseers or bishops exercised no episcopal functions out of the particular congregation in which they had their membership—Lord King on Primitive church, etc.—Methodist bishops claim and exercise authority never dreamed of in the primitive church—Primitive bishops were commanded to " feed the flock"—Six bishops can not, if they would, feed the Methodist flock; as it is too large—When did the primitive bishops hold a general conference to make prudential rules?—Methodist churches have no voice in choosing their pastors—There were no such bishops, as the six, in the early days of Methodism—John Wesley no bishop—Mr. Wesley's letter to Asbury.

THOMAS A. MORRIS, D. D. :

My Dear Sir—I now come to the Bishops of the Methodist Episcopal Church. Speaking of your bishops as the " appointing power," you say, on page 54th of your little book :

" This pertains to the general superintendency. We have now six bishops, neither of which claims any local diocese. They are jointly responsible for the oversight of the whole connection ; they divide it into six parts, each taking his route for one year, and then changing, that each in his turn presides in all the con-

8

ferences. One of our official duties is to fix the appointments of the preachers, under certain rules of limitation well understood among us. In our peculiar organization many individual rights are relinquished for the general good. Ministers relinquish any real or supposed rights of preference for places, with the understanding that the members are not to choose their pastors, but to receive whomsoever are sent. This is as fair for one party as the other. Of course the execution of such a system requires the agency of a third party, the bishops."

Well, Bishop, thou hast well said that the system of Methodism is *peculiar;* and though you do not claim divine authority for it, I am sure you will not complain if I compare Methodist bishops with the bishops or overseers of the primitive church.

In the days of the Apostles there were *episkopoi* ordained in every congregation, and King James' translators have given us in the common version "bishops," whereas the Greek word *episkopoi* simply means "overseers," and should be so rendered, upon the authority of the learned world. But such a translation would spoil your peculiar system as regards the six bishops.

Let us take the following example. Paul

sent to Ephesus, from Miletus, and called the elders of the church (*presbuterous*) and delivered to them his final charge, assuring them that they should see his face no more; and he said to them, "Take heed, therefore, unto yourselves, and to all the flock over the which the Holy Ghost hath made you overseers (*episkopous*), to feed the church of God, which he hath purchased with his own blood," Acts xx. 28.

Now, we are not informed how many overseers there were in the church at Ephesus, but we are told at the 17th verse, that they were all "presbyters" (*presbuterous*), and therefore the "flock of God" which they were charged to feed and oversee was simply the congregation located in the city of Ephesus. The Greek word which our translators have rendered "overseers," in the above text, and very properly so, is *episkopous*, the same which they generally translate by the term "bishops."

While, then, your bishops have no "local diocese," but have under their charge separately and jointly the thousands of your societies; the primitive overseers or bishops were local, and exercised their episcopal functions, if they had any, only in the individual congregations, of which they were members respectively, and to whom they were amenable for their conduct as Christian men.

Take another example in proof of our position. "Paul and Timotheus, the servants of Jesus Christ, to all the saints in Christ Jesus which are at Philippi, with the bishops and deacons;" Phil. i. 1.

Now you know, Doctor, that the Greek word here rendered "bishops," is *episkopoi*, in the plural, and should be rendered, as in the other example, "Overseers." This proves that there were in the church at Philippi two or more overseers, or bishops, and consequently our position is correct.

Lord King, in his book on the "primitive church," after attempting to prove by the early Christian fathers that there was but one bishop, ruling at the same time in each congregation, he proceeds in chapter second to prove that no bishop in the primitive church had more than one congregation under his oversight. He says:

"Having in the former chapter shown that there was but one bishop to a church, we shall in this, evidence that there was but one church to a bishop, which will appear from this single consideration, viz: that the ancient dioceses are never said to contain churches, in the plural, but only a church, in the singular." * * *

"This was a common name whereby a bishop's care was denominated, the bishop himself being usually called the bishop of this, or that church, as Tertullian saith, that Pollycarp was ordained bishop of the church of Smyrna. As for the word "*diocese*," by which the bishop's flock is now usually expressed, I do not remember that ever I found it so used in this sense by any of the ancients."

His lordship next proceeds to give his reasons for preferring the word *parish* to *diocese*, and says he finds it so used several hundred times in Eusebius' Ecclesiastical History; and he continues:

"It is usual there to read of the bishops of the parish of Alexandria, of the parish of Athens, of the parish of Carthage, and so of the bishops of the parishes of several other churches; by the term denoting the very same that we now call a parish, viz.: a competent number of Christians dwelling near together, having one bishop, pastor or minister set over them, with whom they all met at one time to worship and serve God. * * * So that a parish is the same as a particular church, or a single congregation." Page 31.

Again, on page 33, his lordship says: "The bishop had but one altar or communion table in his whole diocese, at which his whole flock received the sacrament from him. At this altar the bishop administered the sacrament to his whole flock at one time. * * * And thus it was in Justin Martyr's days ; the bishop's whole diocese met together on Sunday, when the bishop gave them the eucharist ; and if any were absent, he sent it to them by the deacons."

Much more of the same kind of testimony might be given from this learned author, who was a zealous Episcopalian, and of course can not be accused of any leaning to our view of the subject ; but we have quoted enough to show that Lord King and all the early fathers were opposed to Episcopacy, as developed in your peculiar system of Methodism.

I will now pay my respects to the bishops of the M. E. Church, in all kindness and humility, and see how they will compare with the bishops or overseers of the primitive church. You tell us in your little book, as already quoted, that you "have now six bishops, neither of whom claims any local diocese. They are jointly responsible for the oversight of the whole connection," etc.

From this it is evident that you, Bishop Morris, and your five Episcopal associates, claim and exercise authority and power never dreamed of by the bishops or overseers of the primitive church. They only exercised their office in a single congregation in which they respectively had their membership, while you exercise Episcopal authority and power, from Maine to Texas, and from New York to the Pacific coast, every where where your peculiar societies exist ! This arrangement gives nearly six States to the bishop, with a good slice of territory. This puts it entirely out of your power to obey the command of God to the primitive bishops, to "feed the flock of God." Your field is too large for such a work, even if you were disposed to do it.

5. But if I understand you, my dear bishop, it is no part of your business to "feed the flock." Your time is all occupied with other matters, such as "presiding in all the Annual Conferences," "fixing the appointments of all the preachers," and "presiding in the General Conferences," where you make all your "prudential rules and regulations," modifying such as are found to need changing, and abolishing altogether such as are found by actual experiment not to *"work well."* In these General Conferences you have your Discipline to amend, by modifying some of its parts, leaving out a chapter, and inserting one in its place, where your experience and observation •may decide such change necessary.

These duties are arduous, but it being a part
of your peculiar system, you must devote yourselves to them.   Indeed, according to your own
showing, your peculiar system could not exist
one hour without this element.   And yet such
matters constituted no part of the work of the
New Testament bishops.   Where and when did
bishop Paul, or bishop Peter, John or James
preside in an annual conference ?   Or a General Conference, to make "prudential rules and
regulations" for the church of Christ, or to
modify the law of the Lord, to strike out a chapter of the New Testament, and insert one in its
place ?   When and where did any one of the
bishops of the primitive church meet in an
annual Conference "to fix the appointments of
the preachers."   You are compelled to answer,
"Nowhere! never!"

We are then forced to the conclusion that you
are not such bishops as the Holy Spirit constituted "overseers" in the primitive church.
But do you not, as bishops, in "fixing the appointment of your preachers," exercise a sort of
lordship over them, that is wholly inconsistent
with Christian liberty ?   Your preachers have
no voice in their appointments.   To one, you say,
"Go, and he goeth, to another, come, and he
cometh," and to your servants, generally, "Do
this thing, and they do it."

In like manner the societies have no voice in this matter. You say to them, "Receive this preacher," and they are compelled to accept him as their pastor, no matter how much they may feel opposed to him. Thus all individual rights, both in preachers and people, are given up; and your Episcopal will becomes the *absolute law in the case*, to which all must bow with the most implicit obedience, "not answering again."

But Mr. John Wesley, whom you all acknowledge as the "father of Methodism," was not only not a bishop himself, but he was entirely opposed to the whole thing, as his writings abundantly show. Mr. Inskip says:

"In ordaining or appointing Dr. Coke and Mr. Asbury to be Superintendents to govern the societies in America, Mr. Wesley, justice compels us to say, had no sympathy with the high prerogatives sometimes claimed for the episcopacy. He evidently understood the office to be one of supervision or oversight. In other words, the superintendency to which he promoted these men, was *merely an office* and not a *ministerial order* in the church. * * * He despised every thing like high-sounding names and titles. Hence in the credentials which he furnished Dr. Coke, he and Mr. Asbury were proclaimed *joint superintendents.* He used the term "Superintendents," because it conveyed an idea of the *office* to which these men were elevated ; and because of his aversion to the title of *bishop."* (Inskip, pp. 47, 48.)

But to give the reader a clear conception of Mr. Wesley's views of the Episcopal dignity, we shall here insert an extract of Mr. Wesley's letter to Mr. Asbury upon the subject. From the date of this letter, we see that Methodism had been in existance more than half a century without a bishop, unless Dr. Coke and F. Asbury may be so considered. But here is the letter of Mr. Wesley. (See Wesley's Works, Vol. 7, p. 189.)

"LONDON, September 20, 1788.

"There is, indeed, a wide difference between the relation wherein you stand to the Americans, and the relation wherein I stand to all the *Methodists.* You are the elder brother of the American Methodists. I am, under God, *the father of the whole family.* Therefore, I naturally care for you all in a manner no other person can do. Therefore I, in a measure, provide for you all ; for the supplies which Dr. Coke provides for you, he could not provide were it not for me—were it not that I not only permit him to collect, but also support him in so doing.

"But in one point, my dear brother, I am a little afraid the Doctor and you differ from me. I study to be *little*, you study to be *great;* I *creep*, you *strut* along. I found a *school*, you a *college*. Nay, and call it after your own names! O, beware! Do not seek to be *something!* Let me be nothing, and Christ all in all.

"One instance of this, your Greatness, has given me great concern. How can you, how dare you suffer yourself to be called a Bishop! I shudder, I start at the very thought. Men may call *me a knave*, or a *fool*, a *rascal*, a *scoundrel*, and I am content; but they shall never, by my consent, call me a *Bishop!* For my sake, for God's sake, for Christ's sake, put a full end to this! Let the Presbyterians do what they please, but let the Methodists know their calling better.

"Thus, my dear Franky, I have told you all that is in my heart; and let this, when I am no more seen, bear witness how sincerely I am your affectionate friend and brother,

JOHN WESLEY."

Thus we have the unequivocal testimony of Mr. Wesley against your Episcopacy! In reading over the strong language of Mr. Wesley, we might almost come to the conclusion that he was endowed with the spirit of prophecy. Look-

ing down into the future, he saw the extravagant claims and pretensions of his two *superin-
tenden's,* Dr. Coke and F. Asbury, and their
successors in the bishop's office! When, instead of confining their official acts to a single
congregation, as did the primitive overseers, they
would usurp all authority in the organization,
and claim authority to change times and laws!
And scorning the old fashioned idea of a parish
or diocese composed of a single congregation,
they would put forth claims more extravagant
than the bishops of the Church of England themselves. They are content with a local diocese,
as London, Liverpool, Manchester, York, Lan-
caster, Canterbury, Oxford, etc. But you have
no "local diocese." The whole connection—
the world is your diocese. He clearly saw the
evil that would follow such usurpation, and
hence his earnest protest, and solemn warning!

Yet, despite the warning voice of Mr. Wesley,
and the clear testimony of Scripture against you,
you have inaugurated this fearful element in
your ecclesiastical system! What do you think,
Doctor, the "father of the whole family, under
God," would say to you, if he were now living?
Would he not address you as he did Mr. Asbury—"I shudder, I start at the very thought?"

I hope, Doctor, you will not become excited;

and offended with me, for dealing thus plainly with you, and your ecclesiastical polity. Though I have just learned that one of your brethren, after reading some of these letters, as published in the *Christian Record*, became so much excited, that in spite of the entreaties of friends, he threw the *Record* into the flames, and thus consumed one copy of an argument which he could not answer !

May the Lord lay not this sin to his charge, but "grant him repentance to the acknowledgment of the truth ;" that he may be saved in the day of the Lord Jesus.

LETTER XI.

Paul's experience—Methodist bishops do not have Paul's experience—Paul had the signs of an Apostle—Methodist bishops have not—Can not speak with tongues—Paul's commission—He did not confer with flesh and blood—Methodist bishops do—Paul did not "fix the appointments of the preachers"—Paul defended the gospel, and disputed with its enemies—Methodist bishops never debate—Methodist bishops control the spiritual and temporal interests of the church—General Conference—Christ and his Apostles have made laws for his church—The two checks on the ministry.

THOMAS A. MORRIS, D. D. :

My Dear Sir—On the 63d page of your little book, I read the following very remarkable statement. You say :

" A Methodist bishop has a little of Paul's experience : 'Besides those things that are without, that which cometh upon me daily, the care of all the churches.' Our relation is precisely the same to East Maine Conference and to Cincinnati Conference, to Minnesota Conference and to Baltimore Conference, and so of all the rest. It is our duty to care for the entire connection of preachers and members, and, as far as practicable, have them all provided for."

I acknowledge, Doctor, that I am a little amused to hear a Methodist bishop claiming to have the experience of an Apostle. This is equivalent to saying that Methodist bishops are Apostles !—as no man can have the experience of an Apostle who is not an Apostle. A lawyer has a lawyer's experience, and no other man has such experience. A Christian has a Christian's experience, but a sinner has no such experience.

But if you claim to be Apostles, you should be ready to demonstrate the claim, by "divers miracles and gifts of the Holy Spirit." Paul says, "The signs of an Apostle were with me." That is, mighty signs and wonders were done by him, wherever he went preaching the "unsearchable riches of Christ." Are the "signs of an Apostle" with you, Doctor, or any of your Episcopal associates? Can you speak with tongues that you have not learned? Can you "handle serpents" with safety? Can you drink deadly poison without injury? Can you cast out demons? Can you heal the sick? Or can you raise the dead? If not—and I know you do not claim to do any of these things—then how dare you claim to have the experience of an Apostle !

But let us look for a moment at Paul's experience. He was a chosen vessel to "bear the name of the Lord to the Gentiles, the kings of the earth, and the children of Israel." He was called and commissioned by the Lord himself.

Can a Methodist bishop say as much? Paul's religious experience commenced with his conversion in the city of Damascus. He was a penitent believer, and the disciple Ananias came in unto him, and after restoring him to sight, he said to him, "And now why tarriest thou? Arise and be immersed (baptized), and wash away thy sins, calling on the name of the Lord." And Luke says, "He arose forthwith and was baptized." And straightway, without conferring with flesh and blood, he commenced preaching the gospel of Christ.

Has any Methodist bishop had such an experience as this? I presume not. In the first place, none of them, I suppose, were "baptized to *wash away* their sins;" and especially they have not been "BURIED WITH HIM BY BAPTISM," as Paul assures us that he was, as well as the Roman brethren. (Rom. vi. 3–6.) And you did not go to the work without "conferring with flesh and blood," as he did. You first conferred with flesh and blood in the quarterly conference, and obtained license to preach; and finally you had to confer with flesh and blood in the General Conference, and by the General Conference you were invested with the episcopal office. There is, therefore, no point of resemblance between your conversion and call to the ministry and that of Paul. But Paul bore a divine commission. It runs thus:

"But arise, stand upon thy feet, for I have appeared unto thee for this purpose, to make thee a minister and a witness, both of these things which thou hast seen and of those things in the which I will appear unto thee; delivering thee from the people, and from the Gentiles, unto whom now I send thee, to open their eyes, and to turn them from darkness to light and from the power of Satan unto God, that they may receive forgiveness of sins and an inheritance among them who are sanctified by faith that is in me." (Acts xxvi. 16–18.)

From the foregoing, we see that Paul bore a commission from God, such as no Methodist bishop ever received. And in carrying out the great work entrusted to him in his commission, he endured all sorts of hardships and persecutions from without, and besides all this, "the care of all the churches came upon him daily." In what did this *care* consist? Was it in attending and presiding in all the "annual conferences?" No; there were no such gatherings as "annual conferences" in Paul's day, and therefore he never attended an annual conference, or presided in one, in his life.

Did the "care of all the churches," which
9

Paul says "came upon him daily," consist in
the labor of "fixing the appointments of the
preachers ?"

Nothing of the kind. He never performed
any such work. The nearest approach to it was
in his course with his boys, Timothy and Titus.
Through his preaching they had both been converted, and under his instruction they had commenced preaching. He did not authoritatively
"fix Timothy" at Ephesus, without consulting
his will in the matter. On this point Paul says
to Timothy, "As I besought thee to abide still
at Ephesus, when I went into Macedonia." He
did not, therefore, "fix his appointment," as
Methodist bishops do, but "besought him to
abide there" for a time. (1 Tim. i. 3.)

To Titus he says, "For this cause left I thee
in Crete," etc. He did not fix him in the island
of Crete against his will, but simply "left him"
there, doubtless with his own consent. "To fix
the appointments of the preachers" was, therefore, no part of the "care of the churches that
came on him daily." So far, then, as the fixing
of the appointments of the preachers is concerned, your experience is very different from
that of Paul. According to your own statement, the "care of all the Methodist churches"
that comes daily upon you and your five episco-

pal associates is simply "fixing the appointments of all the preachers," and in this way
providing for the wants of all your societies—
a sort of care that never came upon Paul, or any
of the Apostles or primitive overseers.

Paul was " set for the defense of the gospel."
The church was every where assailed by her
enemies, and all eyes were turned to the great
Apostle to the Gentiles to defend them.   He did
not decline the contest, but met the opposers of
truth every where, whether they were infidel
Jews, Judaizing teachers of Christianity, or Pa-
gan philosophers.

Instead of having any part of Paul's experience in such matters, Methodist bishops never
engage in controversy, so far as I am informed.
They leave all the debating with those whom
they regard as in error, to the " inferior clergy."
So did not Paul.   He " disputed two whole
years in the school of one Tyrannus."   That
was a very long debate, but it was very profitable to the cause of Christ, as by that means all
the people in a large district of country had the
opportunity of hearing the gospel.   Have you
ever had any such experience as this, Doctor?
I presume you have not.

I take the following item from your Discipline,
chapter 4th, section 1st, "on the election and

consecration of bishops, and their duties." In answer to the question, "What are the duties of a bishop?" you answer, "To oversee the spiritual and temporal business of our church."

From this statement it appears that you have the vast temporal and spiritual interests of your widespread connection entirely under your control and supervision. You tell us that your church property is worth *twenty millions of dollars.* Then you and your five associates have the management and control of this large property. In addition to this, you have to provide spiritual food for a million of Methodists, scattered over these lands. This you do by "fixing the appointments of all your preachers," so that all your societies, the poor and the rich, may enjoy the ministrations of your preachers.

These are cares to which the apostle Paul was a stranger. And pray, Doctor, what other interests or business have your people? All their spiritual and temporal interests are entrusted to your hands. Then your people are relieved from all responsibility. The church, as such, has no spiritual or temporal interests or business to look after or oversee. You bishops have taken charge of all that matter for them. If your societies do not prosper both spiritually and temporally, you are to blame and must answer for the failure, and not your people. And pray, Doctor, what more does the Bishop of Rome claim than to control the temporal and spiritual interests and business of his church?

In view of these lofty pretensions of the bishops of your church, I do not wonder that a man of Mr. Wesley's modesty and Christian humility should shrink from such fearful responsibilities, and *shudder* at the mere thought of being a bishop. But I must dismiss the bishops.

GENERAL CONFERENCE.

On the 64th page of your book you take up the "General Conference," and say : "Thus far we have discoursed chiefly on the executive affairs of our church, but now turn our attention for a few minutes only to her rule-making department. The General Conference is composed of delegates from all the annual conferences, who collectively represent and act for the entire connection of ministers and members."

In this law-making department none but preachers are admitted. No layman, however intelligent and well qualified he may be to represent his fellow members and legislate for them, is permitted to be a delegate to the General Conference. Is this consistent with Christian liberty? But what are the duties of the General Conference? You say, on 65th page:

"Besides revising the Discipline, they elect bishops, book agents, editors, corresponding secretaries for the missionary Sabbath school, and tract societies, and regulate the publishing interests of the whole church."

I wish only to notice two points in the above, that is, the *revision* of the Discipline and the *regulating* of the publishing interests of the whole church. In reference to the first, Mr. Inskip says, on page 65th : "At various periods as it was found expedient or necessary, these rules and regulations were abolished, changed, or improved; until at length the form now in use was completed." Again, on page 66th, Mr. Inskip says : "The General Conference, for many years past, at each session have appointed a committee known as the committee on revisal. It is the business of this committee to consider such modifications or improvements of our economy as may be desired by the people, or are deemed just and prudent. In this manner, it will be seen our system of government has gradually assumed its present form," etc. And again he says : "To this constant and well directed course of innovation and improvement we are indebted for the adaptation or suitableness of our system," etc. I read the following on the 69th page of your little book. You say :

" The leading men of the church understand her constitution, and will not override it ; they know her true interests, and will endeavor to promote them by revision of rules and otherwise. The Discipline is, upon the whole, much improved recently, and may be in some few particulars made still better."

Do you ask me what these quotations prove I answer, they prove to a demonstration that the economy of Methodism is not of divine authority, but a mere human contrivance, that may be changed, modified, or abolished altogether, by the law-making department of your church. The economy of Methodism is not now what it has been, and it is not now what it may be a quarter of a century from the present time. No Methodist has a guaranty that the bishops and clergy in some future General Conference will not abolish the whole system, and substitute something else in its place. Indeed, the work has already commenced ; as in the last General Conference one entire chapter was stricken out of the Discipline, and a new one written and substituted in its place.

In the church of God, the rule or law-making department is the Lord Jesus Christ and his inspired Apostles. And as they have furnished the church with a perfect code of laws and regulations—"every thing that pertains to life and godliness"—"a perfect law of liberty," no change, modification, or improvement is admissible. That which is perfect can not be improved. Human rules are imperfect, and may be improved, but the divine, being perfect, never can.

The second item, is the *regulation* of the "publishing interests of the whole church." On this item, I wish only to say a few words. How does the General Conference "regulate the publishing business of the whole church?" In the sixth chapter of your Discipline, we have the explanation. The General Conference elect a "book committee,". who are the CENSORS of your denominational press. These censors of the press, have power to suspend any editor or agent, in the interval of Conference! Any editor or agent, who may have independence enough to think and act for himself, is liable to suspension, by this censorship, any day. This book committee at New York, if I understand the system, have to pass upon all books and publications, before they can be issued by the book concern. Thus centralizing all the powers of the denominational press, and effectually discouraging all individual enterprise!

On page 70th you commenced answering

objections to your system. But allow me to say, that I think you have raised some objections, that you have failed to answer, or remove. For example: Your first objection is, "The ministers have every thing their own way, and the members have no check upon them." This objection you attempt to answer by naming two checks which the membership have upon the preachers.

First, they have to furnish the material of which you make preachers. You say, "Our dependence is on them (the members) for men to keep up the ministerial force to carry on the work." What a check this is, upon the ministry! If the members furnish no more men, no more preachers can be made for the want of men!!

It is like this: A government is accused of tyranny, and usurpation, and the people have no check upon the rulers, and therefore have to submit. But the king or governor answers this objection by saying, "There need be no trouble at all about this matter; as you have an effectual check upon us, in your own hands. You have us in your power. If you do not like our administration of the government, or the laws we make, all you have to do is just to furnish no more men, of which to make governors, legislators, officers, etc., and you will dry us up, as all the powers of the government could not make a governor or legislator, without a man to make him of!"

Very true, but would such an answer be satisfactory to a down-trodden people! Such a check would be no remedy for existing evils, and therefore would amount to no check at all! And the withholding of the young men of your church from your ministerial ranks, if such *a thing were practicable, would be no check upon the present ministry! Indeed, if you were not a very candid man, I should think you were jesting in this part of your answer. But let us have your second check. You say:

"The second check which the members hold over their ministers is in the form of material aid. We are as dependent on them for the means, as we are for the men to carry on the work. * * * Now therefore, if you are tired of our ministry, just pull the purse strings a little tighter, and hold on with a miserly grasp, and you have us in your power."

The thousands of your members who have been under the impression that the bishops and preachers made the rules and administered the government of the church, and had things generally their own way, will surely be satisfied when they learn from Bishop Morris, that all they have to do, to check the power and usurpation of the ministry, is simply to STARVE *them to death*. Hunger is a powerful check. But in order to feel satisfied with such a check, your members would have to forget that according to your *peculiar* system the bishops have control of both the spiritual and temporal business and interests of the whole church, and therefore would not be likely to starve very soon!

PART II.—LETTER I.

SEVEN REASONS FOR NOT BEING A METHODIST.

1. Because I could not find the name "Methodist Episcopal Church" in the Bible.

2. Because I could find no divine authority for your peculiar system of church polity.

3. Because the M. E. Church, as an organism, is not old enough to be the church of God.

4. Because the ninth article in her religious Creed contradicts the Bible.

5. Because she practices "infant sprinkling," as a church ordinance, without a particle of Scripture authority to sustain it.

6. Because she receives into her communion and fellowship unconverted persons, contrary to the teaching and example of Christ and his Apostles.

7. Because she has set up a mere human invention, "the anxious seat," which is not only without any authority in the New Testament, but contrary to the gospel of Christ.

THOMAS A. MORRIS, D. D. :

My Dear Sir—In the eleven Letters, constituting the first part of this little book, I have said all that I design to say at present, by way of reviewing your book, on the "Polity of the M. E. Church ;" and I now propose to write a few letters, before closing the series, giving you some of my reasons for not being a METHODIST. I shall *assume* that you are anxious to know my reasons, though you have not publicly asked for them, and perhaps my reasons are not necessary for your own edification and comfort: yet I have no doubt they will be read with interest by thousands, in and out of the M. E. Church, and I am not without hope that I can make the subject interesting even to Bishop Morris. I beseech you, therefore, to hear me patiently.

1. My first reason is, "*Because I could not find the name, 'Methodist Episcopal Church,' in the Bible.*" But before I examine this reason, I wish to say, I am not unfriendly to the M. E. Church, nor do I consider it destitute of piety and moral worth. On the contrary, I have no doubt you have a great many good and pious men and women among your membership. You have also numbers, wealth, talents and learning in your organism. And in your communion I number many *personal* and dear friends, and some relatives. What I shall say in these letters must not, therefore, be regarded as *personal*; but all must be understood as applying to the system, and not to those who profess it; and I assure you, my dear Doctor, that if I could have been satisfied that the M. E. Church was the church of God, I should have gone into her communion with much pleasure. But I will not detain you longer from my *reasons*.

I know that it is sometimes said, "there is nothing in a name." And if you take that view of the subject, I presume you will think my first reason wholly insufficient. But viewing the matter from my stand-point, it is a good and valid reason.

The world is governed by names. Was there nothing in the names " Whig" and " Tory," in the days of the American Revolution ? Is there no importance in the names " Democrat," " Republican" and " Abolitionist," as used by politicians North and South in the present day ? You will admit that these names mean a great deal. Is there nothing in the names " Arian," " Socinian," " Pelagian," " Calvinist" and " Arminian ?" Some of these names had an awful significance in the days of Constantine.

And is there nothing in the modern names, "Methodist," "Baptist," "Presbyterian," "Quaker," "Universalist" and "Campbellite ?" This last name has been given to a large and influential body of Christians by their enemies in derision. And I assure you it has an awful meaning attached to it. The church does not acknowledge it, nor answer to it ; and yet when a preacher of the self-styled orthodox sects wishes to render a man odious in some communities, it answers the purpose just to call him a " Campbellite." At the mention of this terrible name, all the old stories which have been circulated concerning the church of Christ at once start into view, and the man is looked upon as a monster! a sort of Ishmaelite, whose hand is against every man, and every man's hand should be against him.

Yes, Doctor, there is much in a name, as you will admit, and as I shall more fully demonstrate before I am through. Take an example or two. The name "Bishop" indicates your authority in the M. E. Church. Stripped of this name, you would in a moment lose all your episcopal authority, and become weak like other men; and your word would have no more authority than the word of one of your inferior clergy.

I recollect an anecdote of Bishop Roberts, who was a very plain and sensible man, which will illustrate the power of a name. On his way to conference, he stopped for the night where he was a stranger. The family were Methodists, and were expecting the Bishop that very evening, but had no idea that the plain old man who had arrived was the veritable Bishop. A young circuit preacher on his way to conference had also called to stay all night, expecting to meet the Bishop there, and intending to accompany him on to conference. The young preacher was a fair specimen of Young America, rather a dandy.

When Bishop Roberts arrived, he soon saw

the position of affairs, and concluded to remain *in cog.* And no one suspected him of being the distinguished public functionary they were expecting. Being weary, the Bishop retired early and supperless to bed, and was informed by the host that, as they were expecting the distinguished Bishop Roberts there that night, they were keeping a bed for him when he came, and that he must therefore share the bed with a young circuit preacher, who would come in to bed after a while.

The young man sat up till a late hour, having a good time with the young people, and then coming into the room, he found the plain old man duly inaugurated in his bed. So he crowded the old man back to the wall, occupying nearly the whole bed himself. The old man then commenced a conversation with the young preacher, which led him to remark that they had been expecting Bishop Roberts along that evening on his way to conference, but had been disappointed, as he had not arrived. The old man remarked that he was a member of that respectable denomination, and was slightly acquainted with the Bishop. At this announcement the young preacher moved over a little, thus allowing the old gentleman a better margin.

A little further conversation revealed the fact

that the plain, old fogy gentleman was a Methodist preacher. At this, the young man moved still further over, dividing the bed with the old man, and began to apologize for his vain conduct during the evening, of which the old man had been a silent witness, and for having crowded him so nearly out of the bed. A little further conversation brought out the startling fact that the plain old man in bed with him was the veritable Bishop Roberts himself! Upon learning this fact, the young man sprang out of the bed, and falling upon his knees, begged the Bishop's pardon for having treated him so rudely; and remembering that they had suffered the old gentleman to retire supperless to bed, he begged him to permit him to have supper ordered for him even then. This, however, the Bishop refused to do, and gave his young brother a very severe lecture, which he received with great humility.

Now, what was it that wrought this wonderful change in the feelings and conduct of the young preacher? It was nothing that he saw in the old man. It was simply the awe inspired in his mind by the power of the name "BISHOP." He could treat the old man with contempt; but the announcement that he was a Bishop brought the young man to his knees with an apology.

Do you say that it does not matter what name a person wears, so he is a true disciple of Christ? I admit that this is plausible, but is it true? What would you think of a lady who had a good and kind husband, who, notwithstanding, would persist in calling herself by the name of some other man? Would it imply no impropriety, or want of love and respect for her lawful husband? Would it satisfy him for her to say, in justification of her course, "All is right, my dear husband; I acknowledge you as my lawful husband, and I assure you that I am your true and devoted wife; and it does not matter whose name I wear—the name is nothing; I certainly intend no disrespect to you?"

Such reasoning, so far from satisfying him, would only be adding insult to injury. Well, the church of God is called "the bride, the Lamb's wife." Again, she is represented as a "bride adorned for her husband." Therefore right reason says, that as a dutiful wife she should wear the name of her husband and Lord, "who gave himself for her, that he might sanctify and cleanse her, by the washing of water by the word." And for her to choose another name by which to be known, is to treat him with contempt, and show a want of love and respect for the heavenly husband, who is Christ.

I became religious when I was quite young. And before uniting with any church, I examined the doctrines and discipline of the M. E. Church, and I also made diligent search of the holy Scriptures, to the best of my ability, and the creeds of all parties, to ascertain, if I could, who of all the sects were right, or nearest right. I was willing to be a Methodist, or any thing else, provided I could be satisfied that such an 'organism was scriptural and divine. And I knew that if I could find the NAME, doctrines and government of the M. E. Church in the New Testament, it would be right to unite with it.

But I need hardly say to a man of your experience and research, that I searched in vain. I failed to find the Methodist Church, as such, once named or even alluded to in the Bible. It is true that I found where Agrippa said to Paul, "Almost thou persuadest me to be a CHRISTIAN," not a "Methodist." I also found where Peter said to the disciples of his time, "If any man suffer as a CHRISTIAN, let him not be ashamed." But I could not find where he ever told any one to "suffer as a Methodist, a Baptist, a Presbyterian, or a Campbellite!" From this I concluded that if any man should suffer on account of any of these sectarian names, he would have great reason to be ashamed ; that is, if he were to wear any of these party names of choice.

But I admit that I found the name " METHOD-IST," but not in the Bible.   I found it in a little book called the " Doctrines and Discipline of the Methodist Episcopal Church."   And I learn from the history of the rise and progress of your societies in England, that the name " Method-ist" was first given to your people in derision by their enemies.   But, strange to say, they afterwards adopted it as a badge of distinction ! The name is only about a hundred years old, and is therefore too recent to be found in the Bible, by about seventeen centuries !

Therefore the name " Methodist" is not from heaven, but of men, and wicked men at that ! Finding this to be so, I could not adopt it, or consent to wear it, in view of my responsibility to God.   But in searching the Scriptures for the " good and the right way," I also found the following Scripture, " And the disciples were called Christians first at Antioch," Acts xi. 26. They were not called " Methodists," " Bap-tists," " Presbyterians," or " Campbellites," but simply " CHRISTIANS."

Do you say that this name also was given in *derision* by the enemies of the disciples ?   If so, please look into your Greek Testament, and you will see your mistake. The Greek word in the text which our translators have rendered, in the common version, *"called,"* is *kreematinai,* from *kreematizo.* This word occurs nine times in the Greek New Testament, as follows :

Acts ii. 12, and is translated, "warned of God."

Acts ii. 22, also translated, "warned of God."

Luke ii. 26, translated, "revealed unto him by the Spirit."

Acts x. 22, translated, "warned of God."

Acts xi. 26, translated, "called Christians."

Rom. vii. 2, translated, "shall be called."

Heb. viii. 5, translated, "was admonished of God."

Heb. xi. 7, translated, "warned of God."

Heb. xii. 25, translated, "who spake."

This word, *kreematizo,* is defined in our lexicons thus : In New Testament, "to impart a divine warning, or admonition, give instruction or directions under the guidance of inspiration ; and pass ; to receive a divine admonition, be warned of God, be divinely instructed ; in tears ; to be called, to be named, be known by a particular appellation," etc.

Therefore, in strict accordance with the meaning of this word, as given above, and which you know is correct, the passage under consideration (Acts xi. 26) might be rendered thus: "And the disciples were called, or named of God, Christians first at Antioch." Now, Doctor, if you will take the trouble to examine all the above examples, where the word occurs in the Greek Testament, you will find that I am correct, and that it is never used in the New Testament in any other sense than that of a divine warning, or divine direction.

It follows, then, with the clearness of demonstration, that the name "Christian," and not "Methodist," is the divinely authorized name, and was given to the disciples of Christ, by God himself, at the great city of Antioch, after the multitude of the disciples, both Jew and Gentile, had become very great in that city. This divine name, as you know, was received and worn by all the disciples from that time onward, till the grand apostasy. Properly speaking, there were but two parties—the church of God, who were called Christians by divine authority, and the world.

The followers of Christ were persecuted under this divine name, and they were not ashamed to "suffer as Christians." They knew that there was no other NAME given on earth and among men, for salvation, but the name of Christ, and they rejoiced that they were counted worthy to suffer for his name. James says to his brethren, "Do they not blaspheme that worthy name by the which ye are called?" (James ii. 7.) What "worthy NAME," Doctor, do you think it was by which the disciples "were called?" Was it "Methodist?" No; nobody was called by that name in that age of the world, and for seventeen hundred years afterwards! It was the name "Christian." It was the "worthy name," as it was bestowed upon them by God himself. Again, Paul says, "For this cause I bow my knees unto the Father of our Lord Jesus Christ, of whom the whole family in heaven and earth is named;" Eph. iii. 14, 15.

What name think you, Doctor, did the heavenly Father give to his great family? Was it the name *Methodist?* You do not claim this, I know. Was it the name *Christian?* This was certainly the "new name," which the Lord named. He called them Christians at Antioch. Christian is the family name. Christ, the Head of the family, and Christian, the family, so called or named from him. Christ means the Anointed, and as all his disciples receive the Holy Spirit, which is the unction or anointing, it is proper that they wear the name Christian, which the mouth of the Lord has named. I am sure that you can not object to this.

Sectarianism, which is only another name for heresy, sprang up out of the apostasy, and the parties named themselves according to their own fancy. They were not satisfied with the divinely given name of the family of God—" Christian." This was not sufficiently explicit for them. As each new party differed in some things from all the older parties, it must needs have a new name to distinguish it from all the rest. And after the great reformation of the sixteenth century was fully inaugurated and had proved a success, one party of Protestants called themselves Lutherans, because Luther was their principal teacher and leader ; and afterwards the Calvinists, at Geneva, were ca'led Presbyterians, from the form of church government which they adopted. And as new parties broke off from these, they assumed new names, to indicate the differences.

In this way, the followers of Mr. Wesley were called Methodists, not by divine authority, nor by themselves, but by sinners. This occurred while they were all members of the Church of England. But when they separated from that church, they adopted it as their denominational cognomen.

Thus, after examining the whole subject as fully as I was capable, and finding no mention of the "Methodist" name in the oracles of God, I could not consent to wear it. I saw that it was a mere humanism, of no authority whatever, and only calculated to keep Christians divided, and prevent the union for which Jesus prayed. (John xvii. 21.)

But I did find in the oracles of God the good old family name "Christian," given by divine authority, first at Antioch, and which was worn and honored by Paul and all the Apostles and primitive Christians, and all that mighty host of confessors of the divine Savior who suffered martyrdom during the first three hundred years of the Christian era. Under this worthy name, they suffered, and would not deny it. And finding a religious organism answering precisely to the description of the church of God found in the New Testament, holding fast the "form of sound words" and "contending earnestly for the faith once delivered to the saints," and wearing the same good old family name CHRISTIAN, I was satisfied that I had found "the church of God," and accordingly I united myself with her, to keep the ordinances as delivered to her by the Apostles. Was I not right, Doctor?

And permit me to assure you that I have never had any doubts of the correctness of my action in this matter. Indeed, I am sure that we are *right,* and *can not be wrong,* in our attempt to return to the " old paths," and to build upon the " foundation of Apostles and Prophets, Jesus Christ himself being the chief cornerstone." If any thing is right and safe under these broad heavens, it is the ground we occupy. It is simply to take God at his word, believe what he has said, and do what he has commanded, and in the way he has commanded it, and expect the fulfillment of all his promises. The Lord lead us into all truth.

LETTER II.

THOMAS A. MORRIS, D. D.:

My Dear Sir—My second reason for not being a Methodist is, "*Because I could find no authority in the Bible for the peculiar polity of the Methodist Episcopal Church.*"

You will not be surprised at my failure to find this authority in the holy oracles, as you have not been able to find it there yourself. Indeed, you do not claim divine authority for it, but very distinctly admit, as quoted in a former letter, that your polity is *human*. Let me refresh your mind with that admission. You say on page 15th:

"The government of the Methodist Episcopal Church is peculiar. * * * It is eminently practical; was not formed by theorizing, but is the result of experience. As Methodism arose and progressed, where the want of a rule was felt to aid the work, it was adopted. If its practical working was found to be good it was retained, but if not good, it was modified or abolished."

To the same effect, I quote also from the address in your Discipline, as follows: "We esteem it our duty and privilege most earnestly to recommend to you, as members of our church, our FORM OF DISCIPLINE, which has been founded on the experience of a long series of years ; as also on the observations and remarks we have made on ancient and modern churches.'' (Dis. page 5th.)

From these testimonies it is evident that you do not regard your peculiar polity as of divine authority, but an experiment founded, not upon the Bible, or drawn from the Bible, but "founded upon the experience of a long series of years, and also on the observations and remarks which we [the Bishops] have made on ancient and modern churches." Jesus did not build his church on the " experience and observations" of bishops or laymen, but upon the truth confessed by Peter, " Thou art the Christ, the Son of the living God."

Mr. Inskip, your historian, fully admits the humanism of Methodism, in the following words: " Before entering upon the merits of the discussion suggested in the title-page, the reader is requested to pause a moment, to contemplate the life and character of the founder of Methodism, John Wesley ;" p. 18.

Here it is distinctly claimed that John Wesley was the FOUNDER of Methodism ; while every one knows that Jesus Christ was the FOUNDER of Christianity and the Christian church. Therefore Methodism is not Christianity, yourselves being judges. Once more; Mr. Inskip says, "A more wise or better arranged system of religious and moral enterprise could not have been conceived. Of course, like all other human institutions, it has defects and imperfections." (Inskip, p. 65.)

Let the above suffice. Of course, with the above facts before his mind, no one would expect to find the peculiar polity of the M. E. Church in the Bible. It is not there. "It is peculiar." Neither the bishops nor historians of the church claim to have found any traces of it there, and as honest men frankly admit that it is a HUMAN INSTITUTION.

I could not, therefore, embrace it. And finding that there was a divine "form of doctrine," and that the Lord Jesus had established a government over his church, which was definitely set out in the New Testament, and that the Christian church held the doctrine and submitted to the government of the Lord Jesus Christ, as laid down in the New Testament, received and practiced by the church of Christ in the beginning, without addition or amendment, I became satisfied that it was the church of God, and accordingly united with her. Was I not right, Doctor?

.My third reason is, "*Because, as an organism, it is not of God, but of the fathers.*"

We have already anticipated most that we have to say under this head. I recognize many good and pious people in the M. E. Church, who are no doubt Christians, because they have believed on the name of the Lord Jesus, and have obeyed his gospel; yet the M. E. Church, as a peculiar organism, is not of God, but of the fathers. As such, it was founded by Mr. Wesley and his coadjutors, about a century ago, and every one knows that no such peculiar organism ever existed before, under any dispensation. On the other hand, the church of Jesus Christ is a *divine* organism, being "fitly framed together and compacted by that which every joint supplieth." Jesus says of his church, "Upon this rock I will build my church." The church, as a divine organism, was fully organized on the day of Pentecost, when Jesus, the Head of the church, was glorified, and sent down the Holy Spirit, some seventeen hundred years before Methodism was founded by the fathers.

God is glorified in this church, as Paul declares: "To whom be glory in the church, throughout all ages, world without end." The conclusion I drew from this was, that if God was glorified in the church, he was not glorified out of it—and therefore I united with the church of Christ, that I might be enabled to "glorify God in my body and spirit, which are the Lord's." It was with me simply a question between the *divine* and the *human* organisms. Was I not right, Doctor?

My fourth reason was, "*Because the Ninth Article of your religious creed contradicts the word of God.*" I will here quote the objectionable article in full, from your Discipline. Here it is:

"IX. We are accounted righteous before God, only for the merit of our Lord and Savior Jesus Christ by faith, and not for our own works or deservings; wherefore, that we are justified by faith only, is a most wholesome doctrine and very full of comfort."

As the contradictions are palpable, and can be seen at a glance, I need not elaborate them. I shall only note two contradictions. 1. "We are accounted righteous before God ONLY for the merit of our Lord and Savior Jesus Christ by faith." This contradicts the apostle John in the following declaration: "Little children, let no man deceive you; he that DOETH righteousness is righteous, even as he is righteous," 1 John iii.

Your ninth article declares, as we have seen, "that we are accounted righteous before God *only* for the merit of Christ by faith," while John declares that we are accounted righteous before God when we DO righteousness. Now I reason thus: if it is for DOING righteousness that we are declared righteous before God, it is not by faith *only* in the merit of Christ. All can see the discrepancy here.

2. The second contradiction is still more palpable. In conclusion of your ninth article above quoted, you affirm that "we are justified by faith only is a most wholesome doctrine and very full of comfort." In this you flatly contradict the apostle James, where he says:

"Even so faith, if it hath not works, is dead, being alone." Your article says, "we are justified by faith only." James contradicts this, and declares that such faith is dead, being alone. And you know that dead faith can justify no one. But let us look at the 21st verse of the second chapter of James. Here he says, "Was not Abraham, our father, justified by *works*, when he had offered Isaac his son upon the altar?"

Your ninth article contradicts this by saying that "we are justified by faith *only*." Now, Doctor, which shall we believe, the Discipline or the inspired apostle James? Both can not be true. But if any one has failed to see the contradiction, I will ask them to read the 24th verse, as follows : "Ye see then how that by works a man is justified, and not by faith only." Now I am sure you see the contradiction. The Apostle says it "is not by faith ONLY," and your ninth article contradicts this and declares that it "is by faith ONLY." Every one can see it. If the apostle James had been discussing the question of justification with the bishops of the M. E. Church, or Mr. Wesley himself, with your ninth article before him, he could not have contradicted it more pointedly than he has done in the above passage. I have no doubt you and many others of your brethren have seen and deplored the contradiction. Why then have you not taken the proper steps to have it changed?

My fifth reason is, "*Because she practices infant sprinkling, which is an unmeaning and unscriptural ceremony.*" The ceremony is *unmeaning*, because it represents nothing. Baptism, which is an immersion of the whole body in water, is a very significant ceremony, as it sets forth the doctrine of Christ, and is in fact the "form of the doctrine." The Lord's supper is a monumental institution, and sets forth the death of Christ for the sins of the world. And immersion is also a monumental institution,

11

and sets forth his burial and resurrection from the grave. In this we can see a fitness and sig-nificance.

Christ died for our sins, was buried and rose again from the dead. So we die to sin, and are buried with him by immersion, and rise again from the grave of water to live a new life. But we can see no meaning or fitness in the sprink-ling of a few drops of water upon the forehead of a young child, or an adult. What does it signify? Not the inward work of the Holy Spirit upon the heart, for the promise of the Spirit is only received by faith, and infants can exercise no faith. To infants, then, it is an un-meaning ceremony. To adults it signifies noth-ing. You do not pretend that the "inward grace," or "work of the Spirit," is at all con-nected with your sprinkling ceremony, or that it necessarily follows the rite, at any future time. It is therefore an unmeaning ceremony to both adults and infants.

That it is an *unscriptural* ceremony, I need hardly take time to prove. But I will briefly examine a few of your proofs and arguments in favor of the practice. I now affirm that in every case of baptism recorded in the New Testament, *believers*, and not *infants*, were the subjects of the ordinance; and *immersion*, and not *sprink-*

ling, the action, or as you term it, "the mode."

Your principal argument in favor of infant baptism is based upon the assumption that baptism came in the room of Jewish circumcision ; and that as infants were the subjects of that bloody rite, so infants are properly entitled to baptism. But I answer, this is a mere *assumption*, and therefore the conclusion you draw from it is false. The Old Covenant, with all its rites and ceremonies and institutions, was typical of the New Covenant, and its institutions and ceremonies ; but circumcision was not the type of Christian baptism. There would be no aptness in the figure. Jewish circumcision was a peculiar rite, and none but the male infants were entitled to it. While baptism is commanded to every creature who hears and believes the gospel, both male and female. There was nothing like "*sprinkling*" about circumcision, and consequently it could not be a type of your sprinkling.

But while I deny that baptism came in the room of circumcision, I admit that it was typical. And we are not left in doubt as to its antitype. Paul says, "In whom also ye are circumcised with the circumcision made without hands, in putting off the body of the sins of the flesh by the circumcision of Christ." (Col. ii.

11.) Again, the same Apostle says, "But he is a Jew who is one inwardly ; and circumcision is that of the heart, in the spirit, and not in the letter." (Rom. ii. 29.)

Jewish circumcision was "outward in the flesh," while its antitype, Christian circumcision, is inward, and of the heart. Infant sprinkling is outward, and upon the forehead of the babe, and is always, I believe, performed with hands. This can not then be Christian circumcision, as it is inward and "made without hands." The change of heart and pardon of sins is the antitype, or circumcision of Christ, and is done by the Lord himself. It is true that it stands connected with Christian immersion, as you will see by reading Col. ii. 11, 12.

This being the chief corner stone of the whole edifice of Pedobaptism, and being a mere *assumption*, having no foundation in fact, it follows that the theory itself is false ! Here I might rest the matter, but I wish to examine a few of your principal proofs. You quote the commission :

"Go into all the world, and preach the gospel to every creature ; he that believeth and is baptized shall be saved, and he that believeth not shall be damned." You then ask with an air of peculiar triumph, "Are not infants creatures ? and if so, entitled to baptism ?"

In answer, they are not creatures in the sense of the commission. The creatures of the commission were all capable of believing and obeying the gospel, or rejecting it. Infants are not capable of doing either, as you very well know. But suppose I admit for one moment, just to test the argument, that infants are a part of "every creature," spoken of in the commission, and then let us read the commission with this interpretation, and we shall be able to see the "nakedness of the land." We read it thus: "Go preach the gospel to every adult and every infant; every adult and infant who believes the gospel and is baptized shall be saved, and every adult and infant that believes not shall be damned."

How does it suit you, Doctor? The paraphrase is correct, if your doctrine is true. But such a construction of the commission, so far from proving that infants are the proper subjects of baptism, it proves the awful doctrine of universal infant damnation!! I do not charge you, my dear Bishop, with believing this monstrous doctrine, but I do say such is the legitimate conclusion to which must come from such premises! "He that believeth not shall be damned." Infants can not believe, and therefore if they are part of the creatures mentioned in the commission, then they must be damned !

But the premises are false, and the conclusion wrong. Infants are not referred to at all in the commission, and no infant will ever be damned for not believing, or for any other cause. All infants will be saved.

But you argue that you have examples of infant baptism in the household baptisms recorded in the New Testament. I suppose a man of your information and good sense would hardly rely upon the household baptisms to prove infant sprinkling, but the "inferior clergy" of the M. E. Church quote them as furnishing an unanswerable argument in favor of your peculiar practice. Let us briefly examine the history of these baptisms. There are only four household baptisms recorded.

1. Lydia and her household. A record of this case is found in Acts xvi. 13-15. "And we sat down, and spake unto the WOMEN which resorted thither.' Who did the Apostles preach to on this occasion ? To the women and infants ?— No. To the women only. And the Lord opened Lydia's heart, and she attended to the things spoken of by Paul, and she was baptized and her household. All *women*. The baptism was no doubt performed in the river, upon the margin of which they were assembled. No allusion to

infants. And at the 40th verse they are called "brethren," not "infants."

2. In the same chapter we have the history of the baptism of the Jailor and his household. At 32d verse Luke says that Paul and Silas "spake unto him (the Jailor) the word of the Lord, and to all that were in his house." Sensible men do not preach to infants; hence we must conclude that this household were all capable of hearing and believing the gospel. And after their baptism Luke says, "He rejoiced, believing in God, with all his house." From this it is evident there were no infants among them, for they all believed, and all rejoiced with the Jailor.

3. The next case is that of Cornelius, recorded in 10th chapter of Acts. There is no mention of infants in this household, but on the contrary they are spoken of as "hearing," "believing." "The Holy Spirit fell on all them that heard the word." They "spake with tongues and magnified God." Infants never *speak with tongues.* "They prayed him to tarry certain days." Infants never do so. There was, therefore, no infants in this household.

4. The last case is the "household of Stephanus." Concerning the baptism of this household we know but little. Paul refers to it twice, 1 Cor. i. 16 and 1 Cor. xvi. 15. In the first he

simply says he "baptized the household of Stephanus." And in the last place he says, " I beseech you, brethren, (ye know the house of Stephanus, that it is the first fruits of Achaia, and that they have addicted themselves to the ministry of the saints,) that ye submit yourselves unto such, and to every one that helpeth with us, and laboreth."

Infants are not in the habit of " addicting themselves to the ministry," nor do they help with the Apostles and labor in the gospel. This household all did; therefore there were no infants in it. Men do not submit themselves to infants; yet Paul exhorted the brethren at Corinth to "submit themselves" to this household: therefore there were no infants in it.

LETTER III.

THOMAS A. MORRIS, D. D.:

My Dear Sir—My sixth reason for not being a Methodist is, "*Because the M. E Church receives into her communion and fellowship unconverted persons, contrary to the Scriptures.*" That this objection to your church polity is well taken, must be apparent to every candid reader who will carefully examine the following facts and testimony. Your church is made up of three very distinct classes of members, as follow :

1. Those who profess to have been *converted* to God, and to enjoy the pardon of sins through the blood of Jesus Christ. Such persons profess to be "justified by faith only"—to have the love of God shed abroad in their hearts by the Holy Spirit. And a portion of this first class profess complete sanctification ; by which I understand them to claim sinless perfection, in thought, word and action.

2. The second class of members are your *probationers*. This class is numerous and respectable in all your churches. The only qualification required of them, in order to membership, is, that they shall "evidence a desire to flee

from the wrath to come and to be saved from sin." Those who evidence such desire may become members of your church for six months on trial; and if they continue to evidence such desire, at the end of the six months' trial, they may continue members of your church without conversion, or regeneration.

Your Discipline, the fundamental law of your church, clearly teaches the above. And such unconverted persons may live in your church to the end of life without ever experiencing a change of heart.

3. The third class of members in your church is composed of infants, who have been sprinkled and received into it upon the faith of one or both of their parents. This is a numerous class and become members of your church, not because they are believers, or have been converted, but because they are the children of parents who were members before them. Therefore, the basis of their membership is ordinary generation, and not regeneration—flesh and blood, and not spirit.

It would perhaps be a fair estimate of the relative strength of these elements of membership in your church, to say that one half of the nominal membership of your church, comprising the three classes above mentioned, do not profess religion at all, and are therefore unconverted persons, according to your own records. This, I think you will admit, is a liberal estimate of your membership. And what a startling fact is here developed! You claim, I believe, to have a membership of one million in the world. And according to our estimate above, you have five hundred thousand unconverted persons in your church.

I have conversed with some very intelligent Methodists, who placed the proportion of unconverted persons in your church at a much higher figure than I have in the above calculation. I have known many members of your church who have joined on probation, without religion, and some who have lived and died members in an unconverted state, according to their own profession.

I recollect of becoming acquainted with an old gentleman, a few years ago, at the house of his son-in-law in Kentucky, whose head was white with the heats of some seventy summers. He was a Methodist, and greatly opposed to the "Christian Church," and very zealous for the M. E. Church, of which he informed me he had been a member, if I recollect right, for some forty years. But in the course of our friendly conversation, he frankly acknowledged that he

had no religion, never having been converted !
He said that he knew he was then, and always
had been, an unpardoned sinner, and that if he
should die in his present condition, hell would
be his portion !

I asked the old father if he was not still seeking religion ?   He answered, that he was and
had been constantly seeking religion for the last
forty years, and expected to seek on as long as
he lived, and to die seeking.   I asked him if he
would not listen to me, while I would read him
a few scriptures, and show him the defects in
the system of Methodism, which he had no
doubt honestly embraced and maintained all his
life.   To this he shook his head, remarking at
the same time that he had no desire to hear an
argument on the subject—he was satisfied with
the system, and had fully made up his mind to
abide by the consequences ; and he did not now,
at his advanced age, wish to have his mind dis-
turbed by hearing an argument against it.

And this case, my dear Bishop, is only one of
a thousand of the same kind.   The very struc-
ture and genius of Methodism admits of and
contemplates a large unconverted element in its
membership ; and you know that such an element exists in your churches.   I once heard
Bishop Waugh say, in a sermon which he

preached at an annual conference, at Blooming-
ton, Ind., "I charge the Methodist preachers to
be more industrious—to imitate the old pioneer
preachers in zeal and labors for the salvation of
sinners and the advancement of Methodism.
Owing to the laziness and want of zeal among
the preachers, the exhorters and class leaders
and members have become in a measure *luke-
warm.* We have now near a million of members in the world, *one half of whom are none
the better for being Methodists!*" What say
you, Bishop Morris? Was Bishop Waugh correct in his estimate of the unconverted element,
nominally members of your church? If he
was, then I am right in my calculations.

And I know you will not deny that a case
may occur where a whole Methodist church may
be composed of the unconverted element. The
church may be a sound, orthodox Methodist
church, according to the Discipline and usages
of the church, and not a converted person in it!
It might occur in this way: Suppose a Methodist church organized in the usual way, composed
of some converted persons and some unconverted, as all Methodist churches are. Time rolls
on, and no conversions take place in the church,
and one by one the converted persons move
away and die, and some fall from grace. All

the accessions to their number are seekers, not
converted. Thus the converted element, in
some form, perishes; all pass out of the church,
and leave only the unconverted seekers, compos-
ing the church. Yes, and the preacher, too,
may be an unconverted man, and yet a Methodist preacher—as John Wesley was for some ten
years after he commenced preaching Methodism! But still this would be a Methodist
church within the meaning of the law in the
case.

You may say the case is an unreasonable one,
and will perhaps never occur. I answer, it may
never occur; but still it is a supposable case,
and may occur. It is not a probable, but it is
a possible case.

I could not, therefore, as an honest man, with
the New Testament before me, unite with the
M. E. Church, composed in part of mere seekers—unconverted persons, and which might exist without a single converted person in it, either
preacher or people, and still be the M. E.
Church. And especially when I found, from
reading the New Testament, that in the beginning none were recognized as members of the
church of God, except they were converted and
had the spirit of Christ. Let us look at a few
passages of Scripture that go to establish this
position.

The first passage I will introduce is the declaration of Jesus to Nicodemus: "Jesus answered, Verily, verily, I say unto thee, except
a man be born of water and of the Spirit, he can
not enter into the kingdom of God ;" John iii. 5.

All commentators and theologians agree that
the "kingdom of God" here referred to, was
the visible church, which Christ came into the
world to establish ; and that the new birth is
conversion. This is plain and unequivocal, and
proves that Christ did not recognize any one as
a member of his kingdom, or church, till he was
" born again," or converted. But in the face of
this plain declaration of the Master, you take
into your church a multitude of persons who
do not claim to have been "born again," or
converted.

Again, " And Jesus called a little child unto
him, and sat him in the midst of them, and
said, Verily, I say unto you, except ye be con-
VERTED, and become as little children, ye shall
not enter into the kingdom of heaven ;" Matt.
xviii. 2, 3. In this passage Jesus, the great
Teacher and Head of the church, emphatically
says that, "Except a man be *converted*, he
shall not enter into the kingdom of heaven," or
church. If you had been among the disciples
on that interesting occasion, with your present

views, and zeal for the traditions of the fathers, would you not have said to the Lord, " Blessed Master, are you not a little mistaken ? Our fathers have adopted, as a 'prudential regulation,' the plan of taking into our church all persons who 'desire to flee from the wrath to come, and be saved from sin,' unconverted *seekers*, and we have found that it was a '*capital hit.*' But according to your teaching, dear Lord, one-half of our membership is *unchurched !*" But Jesus says, "Except ye be *converted* ye shall not enter into the kingdom," or church of Christ ! So you see, my dear Doctor, that your practice upon this point is a palpable violation of the law of the Lord !

The three thousand additions to the church or kingdom of heaven, on the day of Pentecost, the very day the church was first organized, were all *converted* persons. They all heard the gospel preached on that day, by Peter and the rest of the Apostles, and believed it, were pierced in their hearts, inquired what they must do—were told what to do in order to be saved, and they gladly received the word, obeyed the gospel, were pardoned, received the gift of the Holy Spirit, and "continued steadfastly in the Apostles' doctrine, and in the fellowship, and in breaking of bread, and in prayers." So you see, by reading the second chapter of Acts, that none were added to them on that day, but the *converted* and saved. And you will see, too, that they were not taken in on six months' trial. They were full members the very first day.

Read also the third chapter of Acts, and you will find that some five thousand more were added, but not till after they were all converted. The condition of such membership, as laid down by Peter, was the following : "Repent ye therefore, and be *converted*, that your sins may be blotted out, when the times of refreshing shall come from the presence of the Lord;" Acts iii. 19.

This being the condition laid down by the apostle Peter, it follows that none were received into the church but those who complied with the conditions thus laid down. But I need not multiply quotations to prove what you do not dispute, and what every reader of the New Testament knows to be true, that no one was admitted into the primitive church until he was *converted*. In this matter your church is wholly *unlike* the apostolic or primitive church, and knowing the fact, I could not consistently join the M. E. Church. The prophet Jeremiah, xxxi. 31; speaking of the church of God under the new covenant, declares concerning the

12

membership, "for all shall know me, from the least of them to the greatest of them." If the Prophet was correct then, no unconverted person was ever to be admitted into the church under the New Covenant.

But I did unite with the church of God, when I was converted. Acting upon my own faith, I confessed the Lord Jesus before men, and then I "obeyed from the heart the form of the doctrine" delivered to the church in the beginning. Being thus converted to God, I enjoyed the witness of the Spirit, and was recognized as a member of the family of Christ on earth, not on *trial* for six months, but in full fellowship on the very first day.

This letter is not quite so long as the average of the former letters, but as I can not say all I wish to say in this, I will close it here, and in my next, which will be the last of the series, I will briefly give my seventh reason.

LETTER IV.

THOMAS A. MORRIS, D. D. :

My Dear Sir—I now come to my seventh reason for not being a Methodist, which is the following : *"Because the M. E. Church has set up a mere human invention, the anxious seat or mourning bench, which is not only without any authority in the New Testament, but is positively contrary to and subversive of the gospel of Jesus Christ."*

I am aware that some other sects have used the "anxious seat," and so far this objection lies equally against them ; yet I believe the M. E. Church was the first sect who used it, and by the right of discovery it belongs to her. We shall therefore treat it as a Methodist institution, and an important part of your revival machinery. What would a Methodist camp meeting be without the anxious seat ? It would, no doubt, be regarded by Methodists generally as a very dry and tame affair, not worth keeping up. It would be wanting in what is called the "power of the Spirit to convert sinners." It is, therefore, essential to your success in conducting your great revivals. But I need hardly say to one so well informed as Bishop Morris, that you have neither precept nor example for the anxious seat, in the Bible. And so far as I am informed, you do not claim Scripture authority for it. I once heard a Methodist preacher trying to prove the divinity of the "mourner's bench," by which I will illustrate this point. He said, "But our opposers say to us, where is your Scripture for the mourning bench?" "Well," continued he, "I will tell you; God blessed my soul at the mourning bench; and that is as good as any Scripture." This was the best, and as far as I recollect the only testimony he gave. This was a tacit admission that there was no Scripture authority for it.

The truth is, when your societies began to spread in America, you "felt the need of something" to aid you in your revivals, and you adopted the anxious seat, or mourning bench, as an *experiment*, and its "practical working" was satisfactory, and so you have retained it as a permanent institution. But you know it is a mere stroke of human policy, a "capital hit."

I have been present at some of your revival meetings, when sinners were invited, exhorted, urged, and in some instances *forced* to come forward to the mourning bench, to "get religion"—"to come and receive the prayers of the people of God." Under these exciting appeals.

I have seen scores, of both sexes, rush to the altar to be prayed for, under the vague impression that these good people were in some sense intercessors or mediators between them and God. At the anxious seat they were told by the preachers, and others, that the moment they would give up their hearts to God, they would experience the change called "getting religion." I have known these poor honest creatures to remain in the altar for many hours, praying and agonizing themselves and being prayed for by their honest but misguided Christian friends; and during the long struggle, some would "get through," and others would remain in deep sorrow perhaps for weeks and months, and finally become sceptical in religion, and turn away from it as a fable !

How different was the practice of the Apostles. When the inquiring multitude on Pentecost cried out in the anguish of their hearts, saying, "Men and brethren, what shall we do?" the Apostles simply answered, "Repent and be baptized every one of you, in the name of Jesus Christ, for the remission of sins, and you shall receive the gift of the Holy Spirit."

Now, if ever there was a time when the anxious seat might have been introduced with advantage, if indeed it were of God, the day of

Pentecost was the time. And I presume, Doc-tor, if you or some of your revival preachers had been there, when Peter told the mourners to "Repent and be baptized in the name of Je-sus Christ, for the remission of sins," you would have stopped him in something like the follow-ing strain : " Peter, you are certainly wrong in teaching mourners to be 'baptized for the re-mission of sins.' In fact, that is 'Campbellism.' Tell them to come forward to the anxious seat, and be prayed for, and perhaps they may 'get through' that way."

And by the way, Dr. Morris, did not the anx-ious seat, or mourning bench, come down from Rome ? I admit that the Roman Catholics did not, and do not use it exactly in the form we find it practiced in the M. E. Church. But they pray to the Virgin Mary, and the saints, and ask their intercession and mediation in be-half of the living and the dead. And hence the priests have come to be looked upon as media-tors, and their prayers are sought by the igno-rant as a means of grace and pardon of sins. But upon the subject of the anxious seat, I find my views so well expressed in the *Baptist Rec-ord* of June 28, 1843, that I beg leave to copy it, or at least a portion of it. This will show that the *Baptist Record,* the organ of the

"American Baptist Publication and Sunday
School Society," published in Philadelphia,
agrees with me in my estimate of the anxious
seat or mourning bench. This is a part of a
series of articles on the "Aspects of the present
revivals on the churches, No. 6." The writer
says :

"At the close of the last article, I intimated
that in this I should state my objections to
'anxious seats,' as operating injuriously on
the religious character of the inquirers themselves. To this, then, I shall now address myself. I may safely take it for granted that the
religious character of a religious man is benefi-
cially or injuriously affected, according as his
religious opinions are correct or incorrect ; and
this being assumed, I can see great danger of
his embracing erroneous religious opinions,
from the practice in question. It has been already stated, that those under religious concern
are urged to take the ' anxious seat,' with a view
to committing themselves on the side of God
and religion ; and were this all, the following
observations would be without foundation. But
it is not so. They are urged by this act to
'ask the prayers of God's people' in their behalf.

"Now I am far from intimating that the effectual fervent prayer of a righteous man is with-

out avail ; and as far from forgetting that when-
ever two such agree as touching any thing they
shall ask, they have a gracious promise for their
encouragement ; neither do I forget that inspired men ask the prayers of the churches on
their behalf. The danger, in the case before us,
arises from the moral condition, at the time, of
those who are encouraged to ask the prayers of
Christians. Their condition is one of extreme
spiritual ignorance, and of this they are just beginning to be sensible ; the sense of their ignorance expresses itself in the inquiry, ' What
shall we do ?' ' What must we do to be saved ?'
If they put not forth virtually these inquiries,
they are not properly to be considered ' anxious,' and hence the ' anxious seat' is not their
place.

"But if they make these inquiries, what answer do they receive ? ' What shall you do to
be saved ? Ask the prayers of God's people,
by coming to the anxious seat,' says the minister. Now the minister is the religious teacher
of these people ; and he thus teaches them (un-
wittingly, I acknowledge) another way of salvation than the true one. They receive the impression that God's people are mediators between them and himself ; and thus, that there
is not ' one mediator only.' Is this teaching

calculated to exalt Christ, in their estimation, as
the only foundation of a sinner's hope? Will
this teaching produce a race of Christians of the
class of him who, on his way to the stake, said,
'None but Christ; none but Christ?' In such
teaching, I ask, where is the BLOOD?

"But this subject has other aspects. If ministers of Christ will thoroughly reflect on the ten-
dencies of this practice, it will, I am certain, be
speedily abandoned. It may startle some of
them to learn that, by this measure, (not a *new*
one, as will soon appear,) they are preparing the
way for one of the grossest abominations of Papal idolatry to overshadow the land. 'Howbeit
they mean it not so; neither cometh it into their
heart.' I allude to the worship of saints. 'Strike
but hear me,' as the Grecian said. Brethren,
cast not this paper aside, under the conviction
that the writer is mad; but accompany him to
the page of history, and trace with him the actual origin of the worship of saints in the Papal
church; and you will say, 'How like this is, to
this!' Idolatry in the church did not rise at
once. There was a 'day of small things' which
was overlooked; and behold, whereunto did it
grow? But to the page of history is our appeal.

"The actual origin of the worship of saints,

is as follows : In the third century, Tertullian, an illustrious pastor of Carthage, holds the following language in his work, *de penitentia:* 'It is necessary to change our dress and food, we must put on sackcloth and ashes, we must renounce all comfort, and adorning of the body, and falling down before the priest, implore the intercession of the brethren.' Here is the origin both of mortifications, penances, etc., and saint worship. 'Behold,' says D'Aubigne on this page of Tertullian, 'man turned aside from God, and turned back upon himself.'

  "Now I ask whether, so far as the practice in question is concerned, there is no identity of import in the expressions, 'Ask the prayers of God's people,' and 'Implore the intercession of the brethren?' But the latter is shown, by the pen of history, to have been the origin of saint worship : and for what the former shall bring upon the churches, the ministers of the present age will be held responsible. 'Consider of it, take advice, and speak your mind ;' Jud. xix. 30. How natural the progress is, in a mind spiritually enlightened, from 'asking the prayers of God's people,' to the idolatry of the church of Rome, a moment's reflection will convince any one.

  "The people on whose prayers the inquirer

is taught to rely, are his neighbors, acquaintances and relatives—persons whom he knows, from daily intercourse with them, have many imperfections, and are, indeed, very ordinary saints ; and he reasons thus : 'If their prayers on my behalf will be prevalent, how much more so the prayers of ministers ; and if the prayers of saints on earth are prevalent, *a fortiori*, the prayers of those in heaven will be more so. If the prayers of common saints avail, much more will those of eminent ones, as Paul and Peter, James and John ; and especially will those of the Virgin avail. If saints, the best of whom have sinned, can be prevalent *intercessors*, much more angels who have never sinned.' Is not this progress to idolatry, palpably downward though it be, yet natural to a darkened mind ? And who can tell whither it will run ?

" But I have yet another objection to the practice in question. It tends to produce in the after life of the convert (real or supposed) spiritual pride. He is supposed to have become a Christian under the persuasion that the prayers of Christians contributed to his conversion. They were *intercessors* with God for him. But now *he* has become a saint ; *he* is promoted to the office and character of a mediator with God for others. Can he dispossess his mind of the thought that the prayers of saints, and of him-self among them, possess an efficacy before God, *as such;* that their prayers stand in less need of the Savior's intercession than those of sinners, to render them acceptable ?   I had almost said *must* it not be the case, that the searches of hearts reads, in his spirit, some such expression as, ' God, I thank thee that I am not as other men are—nor even as this sinner'—'Stand by thy-self; come not near me ; I am holier than thou ?' And this evil, if it exist, is to be attributed to the errors of his first instructions ; and it be-comes his instructors to inquire to what extent they will be held responsible.''

Now, Doctor, it seems to me that my seventh objection to the M. E. Church is well taken, and certainly well sustained by the logical reasoning of this Baptist scribe.   The anxious seat, in your practice, is made to take the place that baptism occupied in the teaching and practice of the Apostles, and thus the law of the Lord is made void by your traditions.   You tell anxious souls to come to the anxious seat, to get pardon ; but the Apostles told such to " repent and be baptized in the name of Jesus Christ, for the re-mission of sins,'' or pardon.

With these facts before my mind, I could not be a Methodist.   But I found the Christian church " contending earnestly for the faith once delivered to the saints," and preaching repentance and remission of sins, just as the inspired Apostles preached it, and I united with her, and *I know we are right, and can not be wrong.* With these seven reasons, I close this series of letters.   And now may the blessing of God rest upon you, and all who read these letters, and save us all from delusion.   Amen.

Yours truly,   J. M. MATHES.

www.ingramcontent.com/pod-product-compliance
Lightning Source LLC
Chambersburg PA
CBHW030601040726
47497CB00008B/2810